BIGGLES

OF THE

SPECIAL AIR POLICE

BIGGLES
OF THE
SPECIAL AIR POLICE

By
CAPT. W. E. JOHNS

PRINTED IN GREAT BRITAIN
DEAN & SON Ltd.
41/43 Ludgate Hill   LONDON EC4

MADE AND PRINTED IN GREAT BRITAIN BY PURNELL AND SONS, LTD
PAULTON (SOMERSET) AND LONDON

CONTENTS

	PAGE
THE CASE OF THE BLACK GAUNTLET . . .	7
THE CASE OF THE MANDARIN'S TREASURE CHEST .	24
THE CASE OF THE LOST SOULS	42
THE CASE OF THE TOO SUCCESSFUL COMPANY .	58
THE CASE OF THE WHITE LION	73
THE CASE OF THE REMARKABLE PERFUME . .	93
BIGGLES, THEN AND NOW	109
THE WHITE FOKKER	112
THE PACKET	123
J-9982	134
THE BALLOONATICS	144
THE BLUE DEVIL	157
CAMOUFLAGE	164
THE ACE OF SPADES	170

THE CASE OF THE BLACK GAUNTLET

"SORRY to seem unco-operative, but you can tell your Editor that for security reasons we don't want any publicity. Good-bye." Air-Detective-Inspector Bigglesworth hung up the telephone in the Air Police office at Scotland Yard and turned a mildly indignant face to Air-Constable Ginger Hepplethwaite, who was standing near him. "Some magazine wanted to make a photo-feature of us," he explained.

"Anything wrong with the idea?"

"Plenty."

Air-Constable Bertie Lissie chipped in. "But I say, old boy, you'd look top-hole in an illustrated magazine," he bantered.

"I'm a policeman, not a film-star," returned Biggles curtly. "There are crooks who would like to have photographs of us and our Operations Room," he added.

Bertie whistled softly. "By Jove! I didn't think of that. Of course, we may have enemies."

"That wouldn't surprise me," answered Biggles dryly, turning to some mail that lay on his desk. He picked up a small parcel.

"That one is marked 'Personal', so I didn't open it," stated Ginger.

Biggles unwrapped the parcel. A dark object appeared. Everyone stared at it, Biggles included.

It was a black leather gauntlet.

Algy Lacey came in. "Hallo! What's all this?" he inquired. "A present from a grateful client?"

Biggles smiled lugubriously. "One gauntlet? I happen to have two hands. What do I put on the other one?"

"Isn't there a message with it?"

Biggles explored the wrapping-paper. "Not a word."

"Are you sure it isn't one of your own that you left somewhere?" queried Algy.

"If it were mine, I wouldn't be likely to decorate it with this particular device," returned Biggles, holding up the gauntlet, to reveal, on the back of it, a gold Swastika.

"Well, blow me down!" ejaculated Bertie. "Who's your Nazi friend?"

"There was a time when a gauntlet was a challenge," put in Algy. "It looks as if someone is after your blood. What d'you make of it? Have you seen this thing before?"

"Yes," answered Biggles slowly. "It happens that I have. It was lying on the aerodrome at Marham, in Norfolk, during the war, when a squadron of American Fortresses was there. There was the skeleton of an aircraft, too, still smoking. As a matter of detail, I'd just shot it down."

"What an extraordinary coincidence," muttered Algy.

Biggles raised his eyebrows. "Coincidence? I don't think this is coincidence."

"Then what is it?"

"That," answered Biggles thoughtfully, "is what I'd like to know. There's a reason behind this. Maybe, if we have patience, we shall learn what it is."

"Give us the gen about what happened at Marham," suggested Ginger.

"That won't take long," agreed Biggles, reaching for a cigarette. "I'd been out, intruding, in my old Spitfire. Coming home with the engine running a bit rough I looked in at Marham to find out what was wrong. I struck a bad moment. The Yanks were just taking off when out of a low cloud-layer dropped another Spit. No one took much notice. We waited for it to land. Instead of landing it opened up its guns. Obviously, the pilot was a Nazi, flying a captured machine. I went up and knocked him down. He crashed on the runway. I went out with the Yanks to try to put the fire out; but it was no use. Curiously enough, one object had been thrown clear. It was a gauntlet—this one, or one exactly like it. I took it to be the fellow's mascot. He deserved all he got, because the trick was one no decent pilot would play. That's all there was to it, except that the Yanks very nicely wanted to give me a decoration, which got my name into print, much to the annoyance of the Higher Command, who, as you know, take a dim view of personal publicity."

"One of the Yanks must have sent you the gauntlet for a souvenir," averred Ginger.

Biggles shrugged. "Possibly. I don't like souvenirs— not this sort, anyhow. There are some things I'd rather forget."

At this juncture the intercom buzzed. Ginger answered. "The Air-Commodore wants to see you," he told Biggles, as he replaced the receiver.

"I'd better go along." Biggles dropped the gauntlet into a drawer and departed for his Chief's office.

Entering, he found that the Air-Commodore was not alone. He had with him a tall, thinnish, middle-aged man, who rose with a smile of greeting.

Biggles returned the smile and held out a hand. "Well, well!" he exclaimed. "If it isn't the Wizard himself!"

The Air-Commodore nodded. He, too, smiled. "Of course. I'd forgotten that's what we used to call Gainsforth in the old days, when he ran the Photographic Reconnaissance Unit. He finished as a Group Captain, you know. He's now in charge of the Crown Film Corporation."

"Still taking photos, eh?" remarked Biggles.

"Yes, but not the same sort," confirmed Gainsforth sadly. "Making mosaics of enemy airfields was easy compared with making films for a critical public."

A curious, puzzled expression came over Biggles' face.

"By the way, weren't you at Marham, in Norfolk, the day I shot down a Spitfire?"

Gainsforth nodded. "That's right. I photographed the wreckage."

Biggles was staring hard at the man. "What a queer thing coincidence is," he muttered. "Believe it or not, I was talking about that very incident not five minutes ago."

"How extraordinary!"

"Never mind about past history," broke in the Air-Commodore. "Gainsforth has come here with a proposition. It's a Crown Film job, so it's okay with us if you're interested. He'll explain. Go ahead, Gainsforth."

"It's really very simple," complied the photographic officer who was now in the film business. "I've been asked to make the most important air picture since *The Lion Has Wings*. If it's up to standard it will be shown at the International Peace Film Festival at Geneva. A big prize is offered for the best film."

"Good. I hope it keeps fine for you," returned Biggles blandly. "What has this to do with me?"

"I'd like you to be the Technical Adviser of the air-combat shots."

"Combat? I thought you said this was to be a peace film?"

"So it is. But it struck me that the most effective way of showing the value of peace might be to illustrate the heart-break of war."

Biggles nodded. "You may have something there," he agreed. "So what?"

"I want you to help me to plan the most exciting and authentic air sequences ever filmed, and advise generally on Service details."

"You don't mean you want me to fly?"

"Not necessarily, although one or two demonstration flights might be useful."

"Why pick on me? What's wrong with getting a serving officer?"

"No use. The Air Council has ruled out the employment of active members of the armed forces." Gainsforth studied Biggles' face anxiously. "Come on, now! You can't let an old comrade down. I promise you'll find it quite exciting, and you'll be in interesting company."

"Meaning what?"

"Well, Max Petersen, the stunt pilot, is in the show; and the girl who plays the leading part, the Nazi woman who loves war and suffers for it, is the top-line German film star, Thea Hertz. I had a job to get her, believe me."

Biggles looked puzzled. "What's the idea of using a German girl?"

"There were several reasons. In the first place, she's a brilliant pilot. She was a professional test-pilot at one time. Secondly, she's the big noise in Germany at the moment. Don't forget the propaganda angle of the film. Part of the idea of it is to be a popular handshake between Germany and the Western Powers."

Biggles shook his head. "I still don't get it. Does this girl fly in the film?"

"Of course," answered Gainsforth impatiently. "She flies a Messerschmitt 109. That's the basis of the story. You can't have a film without a girl in it, anyway."

"I suppose you know your job," said Biggles sadly.

"Don't worry about Thea Hertz," went on Gainsforth. "There's no nonsense about her. Incidentally, she did a certain amount of work for the Americans during the war. She's a fine actress, and will only work under first-class direction. How about it?"

Biggles tapped the ash off his cigarette. "All right," he said quietly. "But I still think there's something queer about this set-up."

"Of course! Film making always looks daft to outsiders," declared Gainsforth. "But wait till you've seen the finished job. It'll be a sensation. As a matter of fact, it's nearly finished. We left the war-flying stuff until last."

"Okay," agreed Biggles. "I'm no film expert, but I'll do my best."

"That's the spirit," cried Gainsforth, enthusiastically.

II

Biggles' first visit to the film studios—temporary buildings set up near the hangars on a privately owned Essex airfield—did nothing to arouse his enthusiasm. Everything about the place, the curious people and their high-pitched conversation, struck him as unreal.

"The story runs from the time of chariots to aircraft," explained Gainsforth, as they walked round. "Actually, we're having to work on the beginning and end at the same time, because Petersen leads the chariot team as well as doing most of the flying. Ah! Here he comes now."

Biggles found himself shaking hands with a keen-faced, agile-looking young man of about his own build.

"Thea's just coming along," said Petersen. "I left her in the hangar doing something with the Messerschmitt." He grinned at Biggles. "You must think this is a sort of madhouse. Still, on the whole, stunt flying is no more dangerous than test flying. Here comes Thea."

It was with genuine interest that Biggles looked at the slim but rather masculine figure in flying kit that was moving towards them with an aloof yet purposeful poise. On being introduced, he came under the scrutiny of a pair of ice-blue eyes that seemed to appraise him with unnecessary candour.

When she spoke her voice was cool. "I am so glad we have a real war-pilot to advise us," she said in perfect English, though with a slight American drawl. "It was only in those circumstances that I agreed to make the film," she added, giving Biggles another glance, one that held a kind of cynical admiration.

Gainsforth broke in busily. "Okay, everybody. Let's get cracking. I want to run over the scene where the Messerschmitt shoots up a line of dummy tanks. Max will fly the machine." He went into technical details.

Biggles made some suggestions.

"That's the stuff," declared Gainsforth. "You're going to be invaluable. Let's go and have a look at the Messerschmitt, to make sure everything's right, before Max takes off."

"See you presently," said the German girl, and walked away.

Gainsforth led the way to where the Nazi aircraft stood outside its hangar. As Biggles' eyes rested on it, he stopped dead, staring.

"What's wrong?" asked Gainsforth quickly. "Isn't it the right type?"

Biggles pointed to a device painted boldly in black and gold on the side of the fuselage. It was an upraised gauntlet. "Whose idea was that?" he asked sharply.

Gainsforth laughed, unmirthfully, uncomfortably. "Oh, that? It gives the machine a sort of realistic individual touch, don't you think?"

"Definitely," agreed Biggles coldly. "But what I want to know is, how did it get there?"

"The Art Department painted it—on my instructions. Ah! I see what you mean. You saw the original, didn't you, that day at Marham, when you shot down that Boche pilot?"

"I did."

"I kept the gauntlet as a souvenir."

"Oh, you did! Where is it?"

"In my office."

"Are you sure?"

"Certain."

"I'd like to see it."

"Okay."

They returned to the office. Gainsforth produced a cardboard box and tossed it on the desk. "There you are," he said casually. "It's in there."

Biggles opened the box. It was empty.

Gainsforth was walking away, but Biggles called him back, pointing at the empty box.

"That's odd," said Gainsforth, staring. "I kept it in that box."

"Well, it isn't there now," said Biggles in a brittle voice. "What's more, I didn't think it would be."

"What do you mean by that?"

"Someone sent that gauntlet to me by post. Have you any idea of who could have done it?"

Gainsforth shrugged. "How should I know?" He smiled curiously. "You're a detective. Work it out yourself. I must go. I can't hold up production for a thing like a glove. Let's go and watch Petersen. We can discuss the mystery later."

"How many people have access to your office?" inquired Biggles, as they walked on.

"Lots. I don't bother to lock it. Maybe you think I'm crazy, but that goes for most people who make films."

Biggles said no more. He felt there was something odd about Gainsforth's attitude; but it would, he thought, be unfair to upset the film simply because someone had sent him a Nazi gauntlet. He could not believe that the introduction into the picture of this sinister emblem was merely coincidence; but, if it was not coincidence, who was responsible and what was the real purpose of it? Gainsforth, he suspected, knew more than he pretended; but the man was obviously so taken up with his film that he was unwilling to start a discussion by divulging what he knew—if, in fact, he knew anything. Was someone, Biggles wondered, trying to sabotage the film, for political reasons? If so, how far was the saboteur prepared to go?

Biggles decided that before he did any demonstration flying he would get his ground staff to have a good look at the Spitfire—just in case there was any risk of structural failure.

III

The following morning, with the mystery of the gauntlet still unsolved, Biggles was back at the studios, for this was the day scheduled for the final all-important combat sequence. There was a good deal of activity on the tarmac. The Moth which was to serve as the camera-plane was standing near the Spitfire and the Messerschmitt that were to do the "fighting". Two black camera-trucks, looking like futuristic ray-guns, manœuvred experimentally. A fire-tender and ambulance stood by, engines already ticking over. Everything looked real—uncomfortably so, thought Biggles. Even the cans of films that technicians were handling looked like drums of ammunition.

Gainsforth came bustling up, using strong language.

"Now what's the matter?" inquired Biggles.

"It's Petersen."

"What about him?"

"He hasn't turned up. What can the fool be doing?"

"I wouldn't know. Have you tried his hotel?"

"Of course. He isn't there. They don't know where he is. They say someone phoned him up late last night. He went out and hasn't been seen since." Gainsforth groaned and ran his fingers through his hair. He pointed at the sky. "Here come the clouds. The Met. people at the Air Ministry say the weather may break any time now. If we don't finish the job this morning, we shall miss the entry date for the Festival."

"You'll have to get a substitute pilot," suggested Biggles.

"There's no time for that. It would mean more re-hearsals. Besides, he would have to be insured, and all that sort of thing. I gave Petersen everything he asked for; now he leaves me high and dry. Curse the fellow!" Gainsforth started, and looked at Biggles as if an idea had just struck him. "I wonder. . . ."

Biggles knew what was coming. He looked at Gainsforth suspiciously. "Go on, finish it," he invited sarcastically.

"I was wondering if you'd help me out of the jam by flying in Petersen's place. You know just what we've got to do."

"Why should I risk my neck for a strip of celluloid?" inquired Biggles coldly.

"Risk your neck!" Gainsforth looked incredulous. "Don't say you're losing your nerve!"

Biggles did not reply to the taunt. He was thinking fast.

A voice behind broke in. "Nerves? What is this talk? No one would question the famous Bigglesworth's courage." Thea Hertz walked up.

Biggles dropped his cigarette and put his foot on it. He did not like the trend of the conversation, but still he said nothing.

The film-star shrugged her shoulders. "If we do not finish today someone will have to take my place in the Messerschmitt," she told Gainsforth. "I have to fill another contract in Germany in two days. You knew that from the beginning, yet you let the picture get behind schedule."

"Okay—okay," cried Gainsforth desperately. "Don't rub it in. I was just asking Bigglesworth——"

"But why should he bother? What is so important to us means nothing to him."

They were standing near the Messerschmitt. Thea Hertz leaned against the fuselage and allowed a casual finger to follow the lines of the black gauntlet.

Biggles stared. The curious thought struck him that the mystery of the gauntlet was on the point of being solved. He couldn't imagine how. But he would soon settle the matter.

"All right," he said curtly. "I'll fly the Spitfire."

"Thanks a million, old boy." Gainsforth wrung his hand.

The film-star inclined her head in a little formal bow of acknowledgment.

While Biggles was getting into Petersen's flying kit Gainsforth ran over the final technical arrangements. "You'll be in touch with Thea by two-way radio," he explained. "She thought it would be a good idea. Your guns are loaded with dummy tracer that leave a vapour trail which the cameras will pick up. It's quite harmless. Don't forget the camera-plane above you and don't forget to switch on your own cameras. They're mounted under your guns and are automatic. I hope you'll get close enough to each other for the telephotos to register the expressions on your faces."

"I'll get close enough," promised Biggles, in a curious voice.

From outside came the familiar hum and clatter of aircraft engines warming up.

In a few minutes all three machines were in the air. At five thousand feet Biggles flattened out and looked around. Just above him was the Moth, bristling with cameras, still climbing sluggishly. The Messerschmitt, with its Swastika-decorated wings, was coming up below him. A faint smile crossed Biggles' face as he found himself instinctively taking counter-action, and then realised that this battle, unlike the others in his experience, would not begin until both pilots were ready.

The film-star's voice, coming over the radio, broke into his thoughts. "Are you ready?"

"Okay," answered Biggles, and switched on his cameras.

Again came the voice of the Messerschmitt pilot; and at the words it spoke the smile of anticipation on Biggles' face froze into a mask.

"You remember the black gauntlet, Herr Bigglesworth?" came the cold, dispassionate voice. "It belonged to my brother. I saw you shoot him down. I, too, was working on the American aerodrome that day—for the Führer."

"Now listen—wait a minute——" Biggles started to protest, but the voice interrupted.

"I have waited a long time for today, Herr Bigglesworth. What you did to him I'm going to do to you—and this silly, childish film. When I have finished with you I shall drop my incendiaries on the studios and fly to my friends in Eastern Germany. I'll admit I have a slight advantage over you. The bullets in my guns are real ones. That's all." There was a click and the voice plugged out.

With the mystery banished and the situation in plain view Biggles' reactions inclined more to sorrow than anger; sorrow that the woman should have nursed her hatred for an event that had occurred in the normal course of war. He was sorry, too, that she had cut the radio, or he could have pleaded for sanity. For a brief moment he entertained the thought that she did not mean what she said; that she was only trying to scare him; but when he saw the nose of the Messerschmitt swing round to get on his tail, he decided to take no chances.

He was not particularly alarmed; at least, not on his own account; for he could not believe that the combat experience of his opponent was equal to his own. What he feared most was the loss of life that would result if bombs were dropped on the studios. Tragedy of some sort seemed inevitable. And the curious thing was, he could not see that it would have made any difference had his own guns been loaded with live cartridges; for even in these circumstances he would not have used them against a woman. The question was, how long could he go on taking

evading action without being hit? He knew he could
not outfly the Messerschmitt in the matter of speed or
height, for in these respects its performance was rather
better than that of his early type of Spitfire. In the matter
of endurance, too, the Messerschmitt probably held the
advantage, for if the woman intended going on to Germany she would have seen that her tanks were filled to
capacity.

The combat proceeded on more or less orthodox lines,
and it was soon revealed, as he suspected, that the girl was
not so adept at the game as she may have supposed. Test
pilotage was one thing; combat-flying was another matter
altogether. In the real thing, the Messerschmitt could
have been shot down a dozen times; and Biggles tried to
make this apparent, hoping that the woman would perceive
the folly of what she was doing. But no. Round and
round they waltzed, with the white chalk-lines made by
the tracer-bullets cutting geometrical patterns against the
blue sky. Biggles could imagine the spectators on the
ground applauding the realism of the duel.

It is not to be supposed that Biggles found this being
hunted about the atmosphere to his liking. Diving, zoom-
ing, banking, jinking, his concern began to give way to
irritation. There was this about it, he thought grimly,
Gainsforth would have a good picture—if the Spitfire, with
its cameras, survived.

Once, after an upward roll, Biggles dived on the Messerschmitt from above and behind while the woman was still
looking down for him. His airscrew was only a matter of
yards from her tail. As his shadow fell across her she
looked back and at the expression of thwarted fury on her
face he was shocked and amazed. Such hatred was something beyond his understanding. His muscles set and his
lips came together in a hard line. "All right, my fine
lady," he muttered. "If that's how you want it, come on.'
He threw the Spitfire on its side and side-slipped earthward

like a stone. In his reflector he could see the Messerschmitt following.

There was a stampede on the ground as the Spitfire tore low across the airfield and shot between the hangars. Behind were some isolated poplars. He passed between them, turned about in his own length, and came back. Again he was behind his opponent while she was still looking for him. When she did see him, however, she spun round in a turn so reckless that for a moment collision seemed inevitable. Biggles' lips went dry as he realised that the woman, in her raging fury, was prepared to kill herself if she could kill him at the same time.

In a way, this thought was responsible for the end of the affair. He had no intention of allowing his tail to be chewed off by the Messerschmitt's airscrew. Jinking almost at ground level to confuse the woman as to the course he intended taking, he suddenly found himself confronted by a line of telegraph-wires. He went straight on under them, and then, coming round in a climbing turn, was just in time to see the end.

The Messerschmitt behaved as though the wires did not exist, which convinced him, as he afterwards asserted, that the pilot never saw them; or, if she did, it was too late to do anything about it. She was, he thought, looking at him at the time. In any event, the Messerschmitt hit the wires. Exactly what happened was not easy to observe, but it appeared that the aircraft started to zoom, with the result that it missed the wires with its nose, but caught them under one of its elevators. It staggered, snapping off two posts, came down on a wing tip and cartwheeled. By a miracle it came to rest right side up.

Biggles sideslipped down, made one of the riskiest landings of his career, and raced tail-up for the spot. Jumping down he ran on wildly, for a cloud of vapour, caused as he knew by petrol running over the hot engine, told him what was likely to happen. One spark would be enough.

He was only a few yards away when the crumpled figure in the cockpit came to life. Two things were photographed on his brain: narrow, carmine-painted lips, and the black circle of a pistol-barrel.

"Don't shoot!" he yelled, and flung himself flat, knowing what must happen if she did.

A split-second later the vicious *whoof* of exploding petrol half drowned the report of the pistol. With his hands over his face Biggles backed away from the fearful heat. There was nothing he could do. The fire-tender and ambulance raced up. There was nothing they could do, either.

Sick at heart, Biggles turned and walked away.

IV

"A wonderful film. You deserved to win the Geneva prize. I think it justifies us in withholding the true story of Thea Hertz." The speaker was Air-Commodore Raymond, and he was talking, in a subdued voice, to Group-Captain "Wizard" Gainsforth. The scene was a box in a West End cinema.

The lights came up, revealing also Biggles and his assistants.

"You know," said Biggles thoughtfully, looking at Gainsforth, "there are still one or two points about this business that I don't understand. You know the answers. Isn't it about time you came out with them?"

Gainsforth considered the end of his cigarette. "Perhaps you're right," he agreed. "I suppose I owe you an explanation, after what happened." He looked at the Air-Commodore. "If I straighten things out, have I your word for it that it won't go any further?"

"Provided you haven't broken the law."

"I haven't done that—at least, I don't think so," an-

swered Gainsforth. He went on. "First of all, you must
understand that in my line of business the film comes
first. To achieve success, almost any risk is worth while.
Maybe you won't agree, but that's how we see it. For
reasons which I tried to explain, I wanted Thea Hertz in
the picture. I knew she was the sister of the man Biggles
shot down that day at Marham. Thea knew he was the
man, too, because she happened to be there, officially working for the Americans, but actually a Nazi spy. Incidentally, she must have seen me pick up that gauntlet. When
I offered the contract to Thea she agreed to accept on the
understanding that an expert directed the combat sequences.
When she suggested Biggles, I had an idea she had an ul-
terior motive, but of course I wasn't thinking in terms of
murder. I wanted my film."

"And you didn't care what happened as long as you got
it," interposed Biggles coldly.

"Within limits," admitted Gainsforth frankly. "I realised
that if Thea found herself playing opposite to Biggles her
anger would make her act superbly—naturally, if you like.
And I was right, it did."

"I see," said Biggles slowly. "So you deliberately kept
Petersen out of the way in order to get me into the Spitfire?"

"Yes. But don't be too hard on me," pleaded Gainsforth.
"As I have said, I didn't think Thea would go as far as
she did. But I was taking no chances. I had her watched.
When, on the morning of the final show, I discovered that
she had some live ammunition, I was shaken to the core.
What could I do? Scrap the picture and throw away a
hundred thousand pounds of good money?"

"What did you do?" asked Biggles icily.

Gainsforth smiled wanly. "I took out the bullets and put
back the dummy tracer. So you see, you were quite safe.
She couldn't have hurt you."

"Why didn't you tip me off?"

"Because if I had, you wouldn't have flown as you did. I shouldn't have got my picture, or the prize."

"By thunder! You've got a brass face to admit that," rasped Biggles.

"We've made a wonderful picture," said Gainsforth simply, as if that excused everything.

"And what about the black gauntlet?" inquired Biggles. "Who sent it to me?"

"Guilty again," confessed Gainsforth. "I did it."

"Why?"

"Because I wanted you in the cast. I didn't think you'd come. Without you I don't think Thea would have come. I knew you'd remember the gauntlet, and hoped that your curiosity would induce you to fly——"

"You miserable schemer," broke in Biggles. He looked at the Air-Commodore helplessly. "These film people are utterly without shame or scruple," he declared indignantly.

"The film's the thing. That's all that matters," said Gainsforth tritely. "Do you still insist that your name should be left out of it?"

"Definitely," replied Biggles. "Publicity is the last thing I want." As the lights dimmed again he got up. "This is where we came in," he remarked. "Come on, let's go."

THE CASE OF THE MANDARIN'S
TREASURE CHEST

"How would you like to undertake a treasure-hunt?" Air-Commodore Raymond, head of the Special Air Police, put the question half jokingly to his operational chief, Air Detective-Inspector Bigglesworth.

Biggles pulled forward a chair. "You can have my answer in four words. I wouldn't like it."

"Why not?"

"Because records show that treasure-hunting isn't the fun most people imagine. To start with, the treasure is always in an ungetatable place. Having got there it's usually somewhere else—that is, if it exists at all. And lastly, you can rely absolutely on at least one unforeseen snag arising to throw your plans out of gear. All most people get at the finish is hard work, with heat-stroke or frost-bite thrown in, according to locality, to make them wish they'd stayed at home. That, stripped of its romance, is treasure-hunting."

For a moment the Air-Commodore looked amused. "This is a very unusual treasure," he asserted seriously.

Biggles smiled sceptically. "Of course. Treasures always are unusual. Where is this particular hoard?"

"In the middle of China."

"Exactly! What did I tell you? Why don't people bury their stuff where it's easy to get at?"

"The choice isn't always theirs."

"I suppose it's the usual rubbish—gold and diamonds, tiaras and bangles?"

"Nothing like that. I told you this was an unusual treasure."

Biggles became sarcastic. "It will be worth at least ten millions, for a guess."

"On this occasion," answered the Air-Commodore evenly, "I'd say it's beyond price; I mean, in terms of money."

"Who does it belong to?"

"A charming Chinese gentleman by the name of Mr. Wung Ling. He's been at Oxford studying medicine for three years, so he speaks English fluently. I've asked him to come here to meet you. I fancy I hear him coming now."

A moment later the door was opened by a constable, who announced: "Mr. Wung Ling, sir."

Biggles' eyes switched to the young man who entered. His face, like his name, was obviously Chinese; but that ended any association with the Orient. Everything else about him was Western. Biggles judged him to be not more than twenty.

The Air-Commodore stood to greet him, pulling up a chair. "This is Inspector Bigglesworth, who may be able to help you," he said.

Mr. Wung Ling bowed to Biggles before seating himself.

"I would like you to repeat the story you told me yesterday," went on the Air-Commodore. "At the finish Inspector Bigglesworth will no doubt have some questions he would like you to answer."

"Thank you. I will do that," answered the visitor gravely. Then, turning his chair to face Biggles, he began. "My story is really a simple one, although there are certain things that will have to be explained. As you have heard, my name is Wung Ling. That may not mean much in London, but in China it is uttered with respect, for we are an old family, old even in a country where age is reckoned in centuries. My home is, or was, at Pao-Tan, in the province of Kweichow, not far from the place where the Burma Road makes a sudden turn to the north near Chung-king. There my honourable ancestors have been man-darins for more than a thousand years.

"Long ago we were very rich, but, not being men of war, when the time of trouble came we gradually lost our possessions until all that remained was our house, our temple, our most sacred treasures, and a little land. When I speak of treasure I do not mean wealth as it is under-stood in the West. As you may know, in China, works of art and, in particular, literature, are held in esteem beyond all things. The golden age of Chinese art began before the Romans invaded an unknown little island called Britain. I mention that so that you will understand when I say some of our art-treasures are very, very old. The great artists have gone, and the world may never see the like of them again.

"Through many centuries, then, my honourable fore-bears, each in his turn, collected the most beautiful things of the land in which they lived—ancient manuscripts, porcelain, lacquer and bronze work, carved ivory and jade. The value of these things could not be measured in terms of money. Gold can still be won from the earth, but if these things were lost they could never be replaced. They would be lost to the world for ever. They do not belong to one person. They belong to all people, because they represent the highest achievements of mankind, of culture, through the ages. They are the treasures not of the present, nor the future, but of the past." The speaker paused as if to allow his words to sink in. They were spoken in a tone of voice so sincere that it was impossible not to be moved by them.

"When the Japanese invaded my country," went on Wung Ling, "with the approach of the enemy the first thought of my honourable father was the preservation of our treasures, those of the house, and of the temple where our ancestors are buried, which stands close. I was then a small boy, but how well I remember with what reverence he wrapped each cherished piece in silk before putting it in a brass chest. He made me, his only son, help him bury the chest in the garden, digging with our hands by the light of the moon, so that should his time come I would know where it was. It is still there. I alone know where it is, for my father is now with our honourable ancestors.

"My father never left China, but he sent me to school in England to study medicine in the Western fashion, thinking that by this I might one day be of service to our suffering and misguided people. Last year he asked me to return home, for he intended digging up the chest. I went. But before this could be done the Communist invasion had started in the north and another war was upon us. The chest, therefore, is still buried. I returned to England. My father remained.

"The rest of the story I know from an old servant who, when the country fell, fled to Hongkong. He died soon afterwards. Our house was destroyed and my father died in the ruins. That is all. I know the chest must still be where we buried it that moonlit night. I do not want the things it contains, for I have nowhere to keep them. They belong to the world, and should be in safe custody where lovers of art can see them and appreciate the culture of my unfortunate country."

Looking at Biggles, the Air-Commodore put in: "Mr. Wung Ling has made this suggestion. If we will recover the chest he will give it to the British Museum. The Museum authorities are willing to defray the expenses of an expedition for that purpose. They will also make arrangements for Mr. Wung Ling to complete his studies and qualify as a doctor."

"That seems fair enough," said Biggles quietly.

"In this matter of recovering the treasure," went on Wung Ling, "you realise that with the country in a state

of chaos and anarchy it would be impossible for a European
to travel overland. It is likely that even I would be mur-
dered if I tried to reach my home. Only by flying could
there be any hope of success."

Biggles nodded. "You're sure you know exactly where
the chest is buried?"

"I could go straight to the spot."

"Would you be willing to go?"

"I would ask for nothing more."

"What is the country like round your home? I mean,
is there a place where an aeroplane could land? That's the
dominant factor."

"For the most part the country around Pao-Tan is treeless
but undulating, although there are large areas washed flat
by the River Shangpo when in flood. The trees were all
cut down long ago to provide the maximum arable land
on which to grow food—rice, millet and barley—for a
growing population."

"What about people? Are there any there?"

"That is a question I cannot answer definitely," admitted
Wung Ling. "There were villages, of course; but war has
rolled over the land, and if no crops were sown, or if they
were destroyed or consumed by the soldiers, the local
people would be forced to migrate or die of starvation. At
the time our servants fled, a northern horde was ravaging
the land, leaving devastation everywhere. It may still be
there. Great areas were depopulated. This, I believe, would
be the case with our territory. Rather than be slaughtered
the people would go."

"Assuming that some people are still there, would they
receive you with friendliness or hostility?"

"Any old inhabitants would die for me, but for new-
comers I could not speak. The only safe way would be
to regard everyone there now as an enemy."

Biggles thought for a moment or two. "There would
be little risk of interference in the air, although of course

I should be prepared for it," he said slowly. "Nor should it, if you will come with us, be difficult to locate your house. But eventually we should have to land. We might find it necessary to remain on the ground for some time. That is really the crux of the proposition. It would obviously be futile to go down if hostile troops were in possession."

"I understand that," agreed Wung Ling. "But that is a factor that can only be determined by going there. If we saw people we would not land, in which case the expedition would be a failure—for the time being, at all events. On the other hand, if the place appeared to be deserted we could go down. It should not take long to uncover the chest."

Biggles walked over to the wall and unrolled the appropriate map. Wung Ling joined him and at once indicated a spot with his finger. "This is it," said he. "Here is the Burma Road. Here is the elbow where it turns north. There is the River Shangpo. My house is about here."

"What sort of weather are we likely to encounter at this time of the year?"

"It should be good."

"The nearest jumping-off place seems to be Hong-kong."

The Air-Commodore came over. "You may find a lot of air activity in that area," he observed. "You'd do better to start from India and follow the Burma Road, which is a conspicuous landmark. By using the Wellington with the extra tankage you should be all right for fuel. It might take a little longer that way, but it would be safer."

Wung Ling spoke. "Once we get to the turn of the road I know every inch of the ground."

"All right," said Biggles. "We'll try it that way. When can you be ready to start, Mr. Wung Ling?"

"Whenever you say."

Biggles turned back to the desk. "In that case I'll see

B

about getting organised," he told the Air-Commodore.
"There doesn't appear to be any particular hurry. I'll let
you have details before I go; I shall probably take all my
fellows with me. I may need them."

II

> "Out in happy Mandalay,
> Where the flying fishes play
> And the dawn comes up like thunder,
> Out of China across the way."

Ginger tried to remember Kipling's famous lines as,
looking ahead from the Air-Police long-range Wellington,
he watched the dawn break over China. There was nothing
thundery about it. Apart from some needle-points of fire
far to the north, where the first rays of the rising sun lit
up the peaks of unknown mountains, the scene was mostly
grey; grey sky above, and, below, grey jungle, with the
river-courses marked with wandering lines of milk-white
mist. As for Mandalay, that had been left far behind,
somewhere to the south.

Starting from Dum-Dum aerodrome, Calcutta, for nearly
seven hours the Wellington had bored its way eastward
through the night on a compass course, with an estimated
time of arrival near the objective soon after daybreak. By
making the flight by night Biggles hoped to escape notice.
For the same reason Wung Ling had agreed that the hour
of dawn, or as soon afterwards as possible, was the best
time to arrive.

Wung Ling sat in the cabin. Algy and Bertie manned
the gun-turrets; not that Biggles expected to be attacked,
but he preferred not to be defenceless if it should happen.
Ginger shared the cockpit with Biggles.

Somewhere below should be the famous Burma Road,

that incredible highway that strides across mountains, rivers and swamps, from Lashio in Burma to Chungking in the heart of China. It was their landmark, their only landmark, by which Wung Ling could take them to his home—or what remained of it. As the light grew, Ginger studied the ground closely, hoping to pick it up. From fifteen thousand feet, the height at which they were flying, this should not be difficult, he thought. Failing to see it, he informed Biggles, who turned a trifle to the north, for according to his calculations they could not be north of it. Thus, by turning north they should cut across it.

A few minutes later it appeared, looking like a piece of tape dropped carelessly across the landscape. Biggles altered course again to follow it. "You'd better fetch Wung now," he said. "He may be able to pick up his position and take us straight to his home."

Ginger went through to the cabin, and was not a little astonished to find that their passenger had changed his western clothes for Chinese, and thus transformed himself into an Oriental in every sense of the word.

Seeing Ginger staring at him, Wung smiled and explained that he had done this for two reasons. As what he was doing was in the nature of a sacred trust he thought it right and proper to present himself at the home of his honourable ancestors dressed in traditional costume. There might also be an advantage in this if they found Chinese people in possession.

Ginger agreed, and having asked him to go forward to Biggles to act as guide took up a position from which he could watch the ground.

With the rise of the sun the clouds were dispersing, and patches of blue sky gave promise of a warm, sunny day. The Burma Road was now in plain view, with villages strung along it at irregular intervals like beads carelessly threaded. A little way ahead it made an abrupt turn to the north. Here the rugged nature of the terrain began to give way to a more open landscape, with much of the land under cultivation, although whether there were any actual crops it was not possible to determine. Across this, coming from some high ground to the north, flowed a broad, sullen river.

A quarter of an hour later the engines died, giving way to a comparative silence that seemed unnatural after the volume of sound that had persisted for so long.

Biggles' voice came over the intercom. "Stand by, everybody. I'm going down."

As the machine lost height, and the ground became more clearly defined, Ginger studied the scene below with more than casual interest, for he did not need to be told that this was the most vital part of the operation. The next half hour would probably see the success or failure of the expedition.

As far as visibility permitted the land appeared to be a vast, almost treeless plain, although the occasional shadow thrown by rising ground revealed that it was not entirely flat. There was no sign of life anywhere. There were villages, or what looked like villages, mostly near the river-bank; but an absence of smoke from cooking-fires suggested that they were no longer inhabited. A patch of white near one of them Ginger knew from experience to be opium-poppies in flower.

The aircraft, still gliding, began to turn. A series of S turns followed, and, finally, a complete circuit. From this Ginger assumed that either Wung was not sure of his position or else Biggles was scrutinising the ground for the best landing area. He went forward to find out, and was disconcerted to learn that Wung, in spite of his assurances, had not so far been able to locate his home. He suspected that the river had altered its course, as happened not infrequently.

This was the first time that such a possibility had been mentioned. It was, thought Ginger, snag number one.

Wung, he knew, was relying on the river to give him his bearings; if it had in fact moved, the result might be serious, for there were no other landmarks. If Wung could not pick out his own home in such a featureless panorama it was certain that no one else could. Tenuous mist still filled the low-lying ground.

Biggles continued to glide. Ginger could imagine his annoyance, for within a minute or two he would have to land or open up again. He had reckoned on being able to make a quiet landing, hoping by this to escape observation; for, as people do not normally walk about gazing at the sky, an aircraft usually announces its presence by sound.

Biggles chose what apparently he thought to be the lesser of two evils. He landed, touching down on a broad, flat piece of ground, that had once grown a crop of barley. That is to say, the corn had not been harvested, and never would be, for it had been knocked flat by wind or rain and afterwards trampled on. The grain was now sprouting in the ear, giving the appearance of young grass.

Everyone soon foregathered in front of the machine, for as far as could be seen no danger threatened. Indeed, the complete absence of life induced in Ginger a strange feeling of melancholy and depression. When he joined Biggles, Wung was saying: "Yes, I am right. I see now where I am. The river has changed, and the trees of our garden, which I expected to see, are no longer there." He pointed to an area of stones—it could hardly be called a ruin—that lay scattered about some distance ahead. "That was my home," he said, a suspicion of bitterness creeping into his voice. "No wonder I could not see the house, or the temple. Everything has gone. This is what war does to a country. It would be impossible for you to visualise this place as I knew it when I was a boy."

"Get the pick and spade, somebody," requested Biggles. "It's no use wasting time. Someone had better stay with the machine, ready to get off should we have to retire in a hurry. Algy, you take charge of the machine. You'd better stay, too, Bertie. Take over the forward gun-turret, to keep off anyone who tries to interfere."

Algy and Bertie took their places. Ginger went to the cabin and returned with a pick and a spade.

"Come on, let's try our luck," said Biggles. "Don't look so worried, Wung."

As the three of them walked towards the stones, Ginger remarked that in the absence of any sort of cover they could be seen from a great distance should anyone have watched the machine land. "Not that there seems to be anyone in sight," he concluded.

"That doesn't necessarily mean that no one is watching us," replied Biggles cautiously. "In undulating country like this there's enough cover in the depressions to hide an army. Actually, this is the most dangerous kind of country to cross unless you know it, because you can't see the depressions until you come to them."

He spoke casually, and Ginger did not take the remark very seriously; but he remembered it a few minutes later when a horseman appeared to rise up out of the ground about half a mile ahead. On topping the skyline the man reined in and looked around, and it was soon evident from his behaviour that he had spotted the aircraft.

Biggles had stopped, of course, the moment the man appeared. The others halted with him, and together they watched to see what the rider would do. He was too far away for his nationality to be observed, but from his robes he was not a European.

The man let out a shout, fired a quick shot from the rifle he carried, and galloped away. This, however, was not the end. Within a minute five more men appeared at the same spot. They were evidently prepared for what they saw, for they did precisely what the lone rider had done.

Biggles, seeing what was coming, had dropped flat before the bullets whistled past, and the others followed his example. From a prone position they watched the men disappear over the brow of the next fold in the ground.

"What do you make of them?" Biggles asked Wung.

Wung said he did not know who they were, but supposed them to be the servants of one of the northern war-lords who were overrunning the country, seeking plunder. "This sort of thing was to be expected, I fear," he said sadly.

"I've an uneasy feeling those fellows are not alone," observed Biggles. "They behave as if they were members of a large party. If so, no doubt they will have gone off to tell their leader what they have seen. No matter. We knew that possibility was always on the programme. The point is, keeping quiet won't help us now. Speed is the thing. Ginger, sprint back to the machine and tell Algy to bring it along to the stones. I'll go on with Wung to try to unearth the chest."

Springing to his feet, Ginger raced back to the aircraft. He discovered that Bertie and Algy had seen what had happened, and were prepared to move fast. Ginger shouted Biggles' instructions to Algy in the cockpit, and by the time he had scrambled aboard the engines had started and the machine was on the move, taxi-ing ponderously over the ruined corn.

On reaching the stones Biggles shouted that the engines were to be kept ticking over. Ginger jumped down and joined him, prepared to help with the digging; but Biggles told him to watch the skyline for the return of the horsemen. This order he obeyed, taking up a position on a pillar that had once been one of the supports of a gate. A scowling face of carved stone that had once topped the pillar lay in the rank grass at his feet.

It was soon clear from the conversation near him that Wung's sanguine belief that he could go straight to the

spot was not working out in fact. This did not surprise
him, for the place had been razed literally to the ground.
Fire had swept over everything. Stones, tiles, and other
building-materials, all charred, lay about in hopeless
confusion, so that Ginger could well understand Wung's
perplexity. It was not until some of the foundations had
been exposed, revealing where the doors had been, that
Wung could get any idea of his bearings; and this took
time. At length, however, he was confident that he had
found the site of the garden. All that remained, he said,
was to find the stump of the mulberry tree under which
the chest had been buried. Fortunately there was only one
such tree, and after turning over a lot of rubble the black-
ened stump was found. This took more time. And after
that the site had to be cleared of rubbish before the actual
work of digging could begin.

Biggles set to work with the pick, but he had not been
at it long when Ginger announced that he could see the
head of a man, apparently watching them, above the skyline about five hundred yards away.

"Keep your eye on him," was all that Biggles said, without stopping work.

Wung seized the spade and began throwing the loose
earth aside. His anxiety was understandable, for it was
evident that if the treasure-seekers were driven away by
an armed force the attackers, seeing the excavation, would
guess what was there, and complete the job. If that were
to happen the expedition would have done more harm
than good, for the works of art, if not wantonly destroyed,
would be scattered far and wide and lost for ever.

Biggles let out a grunt of satisfaction and then called
out that he had reached the lid of the chest. But that did
not mean that it could be lifted. Before that could be
done it would be necessary to clear the earth from the
entire top and perhaps from the sides.

The work was proceeding when Ginger had to warn

Biggles that more heads had joined the original watcher on the skyline. A few seconds later a shot was fired, and a bullet ricocheted off a stone with a shrill whine.

"Okay, if that's how they want it," shouted Biggles. "Tell Algy to turn the machine until Bertie can bring his gun to bear. If there's any more shooting, or if they try to get nearer, Bertie can give them a squirt to see how they like it."

Ginger dashed to the aircraft with the message. The port engine growled, and the machine moved slightly. This brought another shot, whereupon Bertie's gun chattered. Turf jumped into the air along the skyline and the heads disappeared.

Ginger was perspiring from a mixture of heat, excitement and impatience. Biggles seemed still to be having difficulty in moving the chest. Several times he seized the spade and worked furiously, but always there was a projecting stone, or some bulging earth, to prevent the withdrawal of the chest from the hole. The trouble was, there was nothing on the lid of the chest to serve as a handle, and the sides, not having been exposed, could not be reached.

It was at this juncture that the enemy made his attack in force, and from the way it was launched it was clear that the leader was no amateur at the game. The attack came from three sides simultaneously, each party making short rushes under cover of supporting fire in the approved infantry manner. Bullets flew thick and fast, if not with accuracy, and the position became desperate. Indeed, it seemed to Ginger at that moment that the game was lost. Bertie's gun was in action, of course, but it could not cover three sides. Ginger heard several bullets strike the machine and he trembled for the fuel tanks. Suddenly the tail guns started their staccato rattle, and realising that Algy must have gone aft he took his position in the cockpit ready to move fast when the time came.

From this elevated position he became aware of something he had not previously noticed. Coming out of the east, a broad black cloud was bearing down on them with alarming speed. There seemed to be something strange about it, but he was too concerned with the position to pay much attention to it. He supposed it to be a thundercloud; and his fear was that in the reduced visibility caused by the downpour, if the storm broke, the enemy would get right up to them.

To his relief the firing suddenly fizzled out, and this he took to mean that the final charge was about to be launched. Not for a moment did it occur to him that the cloud had anything to do with it. Even when some of the attackers seemed to behave in a curious way, jumping up and pointing to the cloud, he could not think it was because they were afraid of getting wet.

The unpleasant thought now struck him that should the storm turn out to be one of exceptional violence they might find themselves bogged. Opening a side-window, he yelled a warning to Biggles, and his relief was heartfelt when he saw that he and Wung had at last succeeded in getting the chest out of the ground.

Biggles was in the act of mopping his face with his handkerchief. On hearing Ginger's shout he turned and looked at the cloud. He dropped his handkerchief and moved fast. Wung, too, saw it, and his behaviour was even more remarkable. He threw up his hands as if in despair. However, seeing Biggles struggling with the chest, he grabbed it on his side and together they staggered towards the aircraft.

By this time the cloud had so far advanced that it was no longer possible to see the enemy. Whether the men were still there or not Ginger did not know. Bertie, apparently, thought they were; at any rate he was taking no chances, for his guns continued to pump lead, in short bursts, into the murk.

Biggles and Wung reached the machine and thrust their burden into the cabin. They scrambled in after it. The door slammed. Biggles came into the cockpit with a rush. At that moment the storm, with a crash and a rattle, hit the aircraft. Suddenly it was dark. But it was the noise that shook Ginger. It was as if the machine was being plastered with bullets. He had never heard anything like it. Staring at the windscreen in consternation as he made room for Biggles, suddenly he understood. It was not rain, or hail, that was battering the machine. It was a swarm of locusts.

Now, Ginger in his travels had seen odd locusts. He had seen small clouds of them. But not only had he never seen anything like this; it would have been beyond his imagination. It was a situation outside his experience, and what Biggles would do he could not think. It seemed out of the question to do anything, for the windscreen was blacked out with a weaving mass of insects that completely blotted the view forward. The attacking force was now a secondary factor.

It would be futile to pretend that Ginger's thoughts were anything like lucid. His brain whirled. He was dazed by the din, and appalled by the beastliness of the whole thing. He could only stare at Biggles helplessly. Even Biggles looked pale, and more than slightly harassed.

The noise increased as Biggles eased the throttle forward and began a blind turn. Ginger shuddered when he thought of what the airscrews must be doing to the insects. He was glad they were metal, not wood, which would have been frayed, if not shattered, by the impact. Biggles gave the engines more throttle. The noise was indescribable.

Biggles' eyes were on his instruments, and Ginger realised, not without qualms, that he was going to make a blind take-off. He shut his eyes and waited, prepared for anything.

In the event, the take-off turned out to be not as bad as

he expected, at least, in the matter of time. For perhaps a minute the noise rose to a deafening crescendo, as if every exposed part of the machine was being torn asunder. Then it stopped, with the abruptness of a radio being switched off. Light flooded the cockpit. More and more blue sky appeared through the windscreen as the locusts on it, dead and alive, were whirled away by the pressure of air. The same thing must have happened everywhere, for when Ginger looked out he saw that most of the aircraft was clear of the pests. Below, a black blanket covered the ground.

Biggles caught his eyes. He smiled wanly. "Trust a treasure-hunt to produce something out of the ordinary," he said grimly.

Five minutes later, well clear of the swarm, Biggles chose a fresh landing-ground and put the machine down. "I'm going to have a look round before I start over the jungle," he announced.

Everyone got out while the machine was inspected. As far as could be ascertained, nothing had been seriously affected, although signs of the living bombardment were apparent in many places, mostly in the form of dirty smears all over the wings and fuselage, where insects had been pulverised. But this was all superficial. The windscreen and the gun-turrets were wiped down.

"You know, old boy, somebody once told me that locusts would eat anything," remarked Bertie. "I could picture the little rascals gobbling up the fabric, and leaving nothing on the spars——"

"I had no intention of giving them time," interposed Biggles. "I've never been in such a flap in my life. However, as the machine still seems to be in one piece, and we've got what we came for, let's waffle along home."

And there the story of the recovery of the Chinese treasure-chest can end, for the return trip was made without incident and need not be described. Later on, Doctor Wung Ling received a token payment for his works of art from the authorities at the British Museum, where they may now be seen, and this enabled him to complete his studies.

THE CASE OF THE LOST SOULS

"A GENTLEMAN to see you, sir. Says he's come from the Yard." Flight-Sergeant Smyth, having said his piece, stepped back.

Turning from the bench in the Operations Room where he had been studying a set of blueprints, Air Detective-Inspector Bigglesworth looked at the visitor Smyth had brought in. He was a smart, clean-shaven, elderly man, in a blue serge suit that somehow did not harmonise with a weather-tanned complexion.

"What can I do for you?" asked Biggles.

"I've just come from Scotland Yard, sir. I saw a gentleman there named Raymond. He asked me to give you this." The man stepped forward and held out a letter.

Biggles took it, opened it, took out a buff slip, and read:

This introduces Mr. John Stokes, of Downside Cottage, Penthorpe, Sussex. He has a strange tale to tell. I'd like you to hear it at first hand.

The letter was signed by Air-Commodore Raymond.

Biggles glanced round to where Ginger was filing some newspaper clippings. "Get this gentleman a chair," he requested. Then, turning back: "Sit down, Mr. Stokes. I understand from my Chief that you've something on your mind?"

The man sat, smiling a trifle apologetically. "That's right, sir. But somehow, now I'm here, it all seems so daft I feel I'm only making a fool of myself."

"Forget how you feel now," suggested Biggles. "Go back to how you felt when you started off for Scotland Yard. You've come from Sussex, I gather?"

"That's where I live now. I served my time as a soldier, and when I retired on pension about six months ago I bought a little place on the downs to start a poultry-farm. It's a lonely sort of place, but it suits me and the missus. At least, it did until this business started."

"What business?"

"Ghosts."

Biggles smiled tolerantly. "What form do these undesirable visitors take?"

"To tell the truth, sir, I've never seen 'em. I've only heard 'em."

"Where?"

"Up in the air, over my head."

"What sort of noise do they make?"

"Well, the first time I heard it, it sounded a bit like a pig squealing, only not so loud. The next time I heard the thing sneeze. The last time—and I ain't the nervy sort, mind you—I thought I should have passed out. I was half asleep when a voice just over my head sort of hissed at me. 'Lie down!' it said."

"What did you do?"

"Do? I just broke into a sweat and made for home at the double. I was outside, you understand."

Biggles' face was expressionless. "You're sure these noises came from the air?"

"Right over my head."

"How far over your head?"

"Well, it was dark, so it's hard to say; but it wasn't far."

"You looked up, naturally?"

"Too true I did; but I couldn't see a thing."

"Was it a moonlight night?"

"No. There were just the stars."

"You're quite sure it wasn't an owl you heard, or a night bird of some sort?"

"I've heard plenty of owls, but I've never heard one talk or sneeze."

"You've heard the thing three times altogether?"

"Yes. But it's been there other times as well."

"How do you know?"

"Because once, when I was in bed, it picked up a chicken coop, dragged it up the hill and then dropped it in the middle of a field."

"Were there any chickens in the coop?"

"Yes."

"Were they still in it afterwards?"

"Yes."

"When you've heard the thing has it always been about the same hour?"

"Yes."

"At about what time?"

"Between two and three in the morning."

"What were you doing out at that hour?"

"I was watching my hens. As you may have heard, gangs come out from London to raid the countryside for poultry, eggs, and even sheep. We have to keep our eyes open."

"When these sounds occurred was there any other sound —such as might have been made by an aeroplane, for instance?"

"Nothing of the sort. It was dead quiet."

"No wind?"

"Nothing to speak of. Just a suspicion of a breeze such as we get in fine weather."

"The conditions were about the same each time, eh?"

"Yes. It was because the weather was fine that I went out. Of course, I'm not worried myself, but my wife has fair got the wind up. Maybe I shouldn't have told her, but I was so upset at the time that I had to tell someone. She reckons there are lost souls floating about in space."

Biggles smiled faintly as he picked up a pencil. "Can you give me the dates on which these lost souls were adrift?"

"Yes. I remember the first time because it was rent-day, and I'd been to pay it. It was May 28th. The second time was June 20th. It was only last night that the ghost told me to lie down. As soon as it was light I started off for Scotland Yard."

Biggles made a note. "As an old soldier, Mr. Stokes, I take it you can read a map?"

"Yes, sir."

"Good. Ginger, get out the six-inch Ordnance Survey sheets of Sussex."

Ginger opened a cabinet, found the appropriate sheet, and laid it flat on the desk.

"Just point out your home to me, Mr. Stokes," requested Biggles.

The man pored over the map. "Here you are, sir. This is it, standing by itself. It's only a cottage. This is the track I use to get to it. We're about half a mile from the road."

Biggles looked at the situation. "Judging from the contours you're on a south slope?"

"That's right. It's all open downs around us. The ground slopes up behind to that line of trees. That's my boundary."

"It looks an unusually long line of trees," observed Biggles.

"It is. But that's because the trees follow the old road. It isn't used now. When they made the new arterial road they straightened it and this piece was left out, so to speak. There's a local legend that years ago, when people got the wind up about Napoleon, trees were planted right along the old road so that it couldn't be seen from the sea."

Biggles straightened his back. "Very well, Mr. Stokes. We'll see if we can lay this ghost of yours. I shall probably run down and have a look round."

Stokes shook his head. "You won't find anything."

"Well, we shan't find anything here, shall we?" answered Biggles, smiling.

"No, that's right enough," admitted Stokes.

"By the way, are there any mushrooms in your part of the world?" inquired Biggles.

The man started. "Mushrooms?" he echoed. "Why, yes! What's that got to do with it?"

Biggles smiled. "I'll take a basket. We might find a few mushrooms if nothing else. You'll know what I'm doing if you see me about. Let me know at once if you see or hear anything more of your visitor in the small hours. Just one other thing—have you told anyone else about this?"

"Not a soul. I don't want people to think I'm either a liar or a lunatic."

"Good. Keep it to yourself." Biggles held out a hand. "Goodbye for the present, Mr. Stokes. Tell your wife not to worry. It shouldn't take us long to nail down this rowdy visitor of yours."

After the old soldier had gone Ginger looked at Biggles questioningly. "What do you make of all that?"

"You heard as much as I did."

"It doesn't make sense to me."

"Why not?"

"Pigs don't fly. I'd say Mr. Stokes went to market and had a drink too many."

Biggles looked dubious. "He didn't strike me as that sort. I'd say he's a steady, level-headed fellow. Something out of the ordinary is going on where he lives. I'm pretty sure of that, because no incident with a reasonable explanation would alarm a man to the point of going to Scotland Yard. We'll go down and have a look round."

"Are you going to fly down?"

"No. The place isn't far. The car will be more useful for running round the district. You might bring it round while I have a word with the Met. people at the Ministry.

I want to know just what the local weather conditions were on the nights Mr. Stokes heard his ghost. Remember to buy a basket on the way down."

Ginger stared. "What d'you want a basket for?"

Biggles grinned. "To put the mushrooms in, of course."

II

It was three o'clock, and a fine summer afternoon, when Biggles brought the car to a stop just inside the overgrown track which was all that remained of the original main road. The new road, a broad expanse of macadam, ran on, as straight as a ruler, following the high ground. From the junction, where the old road branched off to the left, the trees that Biggles had remarked on the map made a pleasant, shady break across a bare, rolling expanse of open downland, consisting entirely of close-cropped grass. Here and there an ancient quarry appeared as a patch of snow where it exposed the underlying chalk.

"The car should be all right here," said Biggles, taking from it the basket which he had bought on the way down.

Ginger looked askance at it. "Are you really going to look for mushrooms?" he inquired.

"I am, for two reasons," answered Biggles. "In the first place, I like mushrooms, and in the second, as I shall be looking mostly at the ground, it might satisfy possible spectators as to my real purpose." He advanced to the front of the trees so that the open landscape fell away before him. He pointed. "That must be the little house where Stokes lives, down there in the valley. Yes, you can see the chickens. Now let's see if we can find some mushrooms."

He went on to the open grassland for some distance, and then, turning to the right, began to walk across the gentle slope, keeping roughly parallel with the trees.

"Isn't it time you told me what you're *really* looking for?" complained Ginger.

Biggles smiled a trifle sheepishly. "To tell the truth, I'm not quite sure what I am looking for," he answered. "I feel that the Stokes' ghost must have come to earth somewhere hereabouts."

They walked on. One or two mushrooms were put into the basket. But when they had covered perhaps three hundred yards Biggles suddenly quickened his stride. "Ah-ha! What have we here?" he murmured. "Don't stop! There's a chance we may be watched."

Ginger could see what Biggles was looking at, but found little in it to provide enlightenment. Across their path—that is to say, from a point about halfway down the slope from the top—was a rough scratch, or scar. In some places it was a single scratch, sometimes double. In places it was so faint as to be hardly noticeable, but in others it was deep enough to reveal the chalk. It was obvious that something had been dragged across the ground, occasionally tearing up tufts of turf. Ginger saw nothing remarkable about it. Almost any farm-implement could have caused it, he thought. He said so.

Biggles agreed.

Ginger went on. "Had there been only one line it might have been made by the tailskid of an aircraft," he observed. "The double line rules that out, though. Besides, an aircraft wouldn't land straight into the trees."

"That's a reasonable line of argument," admitted Biggles. He did not stop, but walked on a little way and then turned to the right towards the trees. "We've done enough mush-rooming, I think," he said. "Let's have a look at the trees, particularly where this scratch runs into them."

The objective reached, Biggles looked at Ginger with twinkling eyes. "Can you see what I see?" he asked softly.

"I can see some leaves and broken twigs lying about, if that's what you mean," answered Ginger.

"Yes; but look where they came from," continued Biggles. "Farm-implements don't climb trees. Doesn't it strike you as odd that the only place where the trees have suffered is in a direct line with the torn-up turf? No matter. We're doing fine. Let's extend the line from the cottage to where we are standing now and see what's at the end of it."

They made their way to the middle of a double line of trees. "We're now on the old road," said Biggles. "Someone still uses it, I notice." He went on through the second line of trees and paused to look ahead. Ginger also looked, but could see nothing except an upward-sloping sweep of short turf, without a blemish. This continued right on to the crest of the hill, where the position of the main road was marked by occasional telegraph-poles and traffic. An isolated building, too, was outlined against the sky.

Biggles strolled towards it.

It turned out to be one of those modern establishments often to be seen on main roads, where sundry notices call attention to a wonderful variety of commodities offered for sale. There was a petrol-pump. A notice proclaimed that teas and ices were available. Over the door a board announced that Mr. Lucius Landerville was licensed to sell tobacco, wines and spirits. A basket of eggs spoke for itself, as did a row of beehives adorned with the word "Honey". A fingerpost offered tents for hire; and yet another notice, near some kennels, informed the public that dogs were boarded and puppies were for sale.

"How about an ice-cream with Mr. Lucius Landerville?" suggested Biggles.

"That suits me," answered Ginger promptly.

They sat down on an outside bench. A girl brought the ices. Biggles asked her what dogs they had for sale.

"I'll send Mr. Landerville to see you," she said.

Presently Mr. Landerville came. He was a man of nearly sixty, bearded, keen-eyed, dressed country-fashion.

"I noticed a nice-looking French poodle in your kennels," opened Biggles. "Is he for sale?"

"Ah, no. That one has been sold," was the answer. "I've some very nice puppies."

"What sort?"

"Mostly poodles."

"Actually, I'm not quite ready to take on a pup, but I'll certainly bear it in mind," replied Biggles. "Thanks all the same."

The man went off.

Biggles finished his ice and got up. "I think that'll do," he told Ginger. "We'll see about getting along home."

"Aren't you going to call on Stokes?"

"There's no point in it."

"Does this fellow Landerville come into the picture?"

"I think so—unless we've run into a coincidence. His name rings a bell in my memory. I can't recall in exactly what connexion, but when I get back I'll go into it. I fancy I know where I can look him up."

"Where?"

"At the Royal Aero Club." Biggles walked on to the car. "I'm afraid we didn't have much luck with the mushrooms, but it's been a very pleasant afternoon," he remarked. "Quite an interesting one, too."

III

A week after the excursion to the Sussex Downs, at about six o'clock in the evening, Biggles sent Flight-Sergeant Smyth to find Ginger Algy and Bertie, who were somewhere on the tarmac, o ask them to join him in the Ops Room. When they ca ie, requesting to be told why he was staying late, Biggles nformed them that they would not be going nome at all that night. They would, he said, have something to eat in the airport canteen, and stand by until midnight. If a message he was expecting had not arrived by then they would go home, and the same procedure would be repeated the following night. He thought it was likely, he concluded, that they might be in for a busy time.

"Doing what, old boy? Doing what?" inquired Bertie.

"Spook-hunting," answered Biggles, gravely. "For the first time in a week the weather conditions are precisely those that prevailed on the occasions when Mr. Stokes heard uncanny noises over his head. I shall therefore be disappointed if the airborne prowler doesn't turn up."

"But how are we going to catch the blighter, that's what I want to know?" demanded Bertie, rubbing his eyeglass briskly. "Do we beetle about in the atmosphere and grab him by the tail, or what?"

"Nothing like it," answered Biggles. "I have an idea that if he comes he'll drop right into our hands."

"And then what?" asked Bertie. "How can one grab a spook when there's nothing to get hold of?"

"In this case," returned Biggles, "unless I've missed my guess there will be plenty to get hold of. In fact, it may need all four of us to hold him down. That's why we're all going. If he doesn't show up tonight we'll try again to-morrow, provided the weather conditions persist. This is my plan. When we get to the haunted area I shall divide it into four sections, one for each of us. Everyone will carry a whistle. The first man to spot the ghost will blow his whistle. The others will converge on the spot at the double."

"In what form are you expecting this spectre to appear?" inquired Algy cynically.

"As a large round monster carrying a basket," replied Biggles seriously. "He may be armed with a large hook, so watch you don't get an eye knocked out."

"Suppose you stop talking rot and give us the pukka gen," said Ginger sarcastically. "Exactly what is it you're expecting?"

Biggles thought for a moment. "I'm not absolutely sure, so I'd rather not say. But I'll tell you this much, and you can draw your own conclusions. From the moment I saw Stokes I worked on the assumption that he was telling the truth, and that he did in fact hear strange noises over his head at night. When I say strange, I mean they were not the sort of noises made by ordinary night birds. Something was up there, something real enough to put the wind up him and send him to Scotland Yard. Don't laugh at Stokes on that account. Having been a soldier he isn't the sort of fellow to be easily frightened. It's all very well to discuss this sort of thing in broad daylight. Alone, on a dark night, one is apt to feel altogether different. But let's go over to the canteen and get a bite to eat."

"Tell me one thing," pleaded Bertie. "Is this ghastly visitor likely to be solid, or hollow?"

"Hollow," answered Biggles, grinning. "Come on."

An hour later, the meal over, Biggles was just getting up from the table when the Flight-Sergeant came in with a signal slip. He glanced at it, took out his fountain-pen, and made some quick calculations on the back of the paper. "Good," he said. "I've just had a message over the air to say that our nocturnal rambler is on the way. I am also able to announce that it will arrive over the Sussex Downs at a quarter-past two. As we don't want to be late for the appointment it's time we were on our way."

IV

When Ginger found himself sitting alone on the sombre downs, Biggles' remark about the difference between discussing the ghost in broad daylight and on the spot, at night, returned with some force. There was, in fact, no comparison.

The time by his watch was two o'clock. At any moment

now, Biggles had just said, the thing might appear. He hoped it wouldn't be long, because his enthusiasm for the adventure was beginning to wane. The night was fair enough under a cloudless sky; but there was no moon, and the light provided by the stars was not sufficient to enable him to see anything clearly.

Before him stretched a wide, open, tree-less expanse of downs, the ground falling away gently into the valley where Stokes lived. Immediately behind him the line of trees that marked the course of the old road rose up like a black cliff. The only sound was the gentle murmur of their leaves as they were caressed by a soft breeze from the south. The only light in view was on the skyline, at or near the roadside establishment belonging to Mr. Lucius Landerville. Without giving the matter any serious thought Ginger supposed that it was one of those places that keep open all night to supply refreshments to long-distance lorry drivers.

Twiddling his whistle, he gazed into the starry sky. As an occupation he found it more than somewhat boring, but there was nothing else to do. If the truth must be told, he was sceptical about the whole business, and did not seriously expect to see anything.

He heard it before he saw it. At any rate, he heard a sound that brought him to his feet, tense and alert. It was a strange sound, impossible to identify. First there was a loud bump. This was followed by a harsh scraping, with occasional lesser bumps, as if something was galloping up the hill towards him.

For a few seconds he saw nothing. Then, suddenly, it was almost upon him, a spidery object that rolled and twisted as it appeared to skate over the short turf. Darting to one side to let it go past, a movement overhead caught his eye. Looking up, he saw what appeared to be a round black cloud drifting by. Then something crashed into the trees. The cloud stopped abruptly, swaying and hissing.

Startled almost to the point of panic, Ginger remembered his whistle. Its shrill blast shattered the silence.

The next minute was a period of alarm and confusion. A great basket, twice the size of a barrel, appeared from nowhere, as the saying is. From it leapt a man. He started to run, but Ginger tackled him low and brought him down. While they were struggling, a torch flashed and Biggles' voice cut into the picture.

"All right, Landerville," he said. "Fighting won't help. The game's up."

The man broke away from Ginger but stood his ground. "Who are you?" he asked, in a surprisingly calm tone of voice.

"Police."

"I see. It's a fair catch. I'm no bruiser. Mind my dogs."

By this time Algy and Bertie were on the scene. The balloon had settled down and the mystery was solved.

Landerville himself helped them to unload the basket. There were two hampers. One contained a dog; the other a litter of puppies. Biggles satisfied himself that there was nothing else.

"I happen to be very fond of dogs," volunteered Landerville.

"I doubt if many dog-owners in this country would agree with you," answered Biggles coldly. "It was a pilot playing this selfish game who introduced the epidemic of hard-pad that's killing hundreds of dogs up and down the land. But you can make your excuses in court."

"What do you want me to do with these dogs?" asked Landerville.

"They'd better go into your kennels for the time being. You'll get instructions about them."

"What about me?"

"If I let you go home can I trust you to stay there?"

"Oh yes. I shan't run away."

"All right," agreed Biggles. "Do you want us to help you with these hampers?"

"No, thanks. Normally I bring my car down the old road and take everything up."

"You'd better do that," said Biggles. "I'll leave you to it."

Later the same day, discussing the matter in the Ops Room, Biggles explained.

"It wasn't very difficult," he asserted. "When I saw the torn-up grass and the damaged trees I had a good idea of what was going on. Ginger said the marks might have been caused by an agricultural implement, and he was right. He thought aircraft could be ruled out. There he was wrong. Naturally, he was thinking in terms of modern aircraft; but there's an obsolete form of aircraft that most people have forgotten, and it is, incidentally, the only method of air transportation that can claim to be absolutely silent. I mean the free balloon, which for more than a hundred years was the only way of getting into the air at all. Their operators, called aeronauts, became skilful in the handling of them." Biggles reached for a cigarette. "Forty years ago ballooning was still a popular sport. There were aviation meetings, and races in which trained aeronauts took part. Some of those men are still alive. When Mr. Stokes told his story, I was forced, in the absence of any possible explanation, to conclude that someone was using a balloon. A balloon is a fairly simple thing to make, and there would be no difficulty in buying commercial hydrogen to fill it. The question arose, for what purpose would a balloon be used? One would hardly make an ascent in the middle of the night for pleasure. The landing was made near the house of Mr. Stokes, and there is probably no better place in the country. A balloon lands by releasing its gas and throwing out an anchor. The scars in the turf were the result of that. One night the anchor must have caught one of the chicken-coops and dragged it

some distance. Actually, of course, the anchor was bound
to hook up in the trees, and broken twigs showed that that
did happen. Where did the aircraft start from? With the
sea near at hand, and the wind south or south-west, the
answer stuck out like a sore finger—from France. The long
line of trees, with a light behind them, made a good landmark. It was reasonable to suppose that our aeronaut did
not live far from his anchorage. Looking round, we found
the nearest establishment was run by a man named Lucius
Landerville. I vaguely recalled the name. At the Aero
Club, where aeronauts' certificates were issued as pilots'
licences are today, I found that forty years ago two of our
leading balloonists were brothers named Landerville. The
trail was getting hot." Biggles stubbed his cigarette.
"Where was the other brother? France was a pretty safe
guess. I rang up Captain Joudrier in Paris. He was soon
able to inform me that an Englishman named Oscar
Landerville, a dog breeder in a big way, was living on the
coast of Normandy. It then became plain that the ballooning brothers were running a shuttle-service across the
Channel. For what purpose? Well, both were dog-breeders.
Dogs were the cargo. It seemed silly, but not so silly as
one might think. No one can import a dog into this
country without leaving it for six months in quarantine, to
prevent the introduction of that killing disease rabies. It
upsets a lot of people to lose their pets, and some would,
no doubt, be prepared to pay handsomely to avoid the
regulation. That was the racket. The animal-sounds Mr.
Stokes heard were made by muzzled dogs. On one occasion
Stokes heard a voice say 'Lie down!' The order was not
addressed to him, but to the dogs, which may have been
fractious. That's all there was to it."

"But how did you know exactly when the balloon was
due to arrive?" asked Ginger.

"I tipped Joudrier off as to what was happening, asked
him to watch the Landerville establishment on his side,

and send me a radio signal when the balloon went up. The Met. people gave me the speed of the wind, so it was a matter of simple arithmetic to work out the estimated time of arrival. On this occasion we had a reception-committee waiting. Landerville must now be feeling pretty silly, particularly as he was taking big risks for comparatively small profits. Of course, the profit angle may not have been everything. Once an airman always an airman is an old saying; and one of the curious facts of aviation is the contempt the lighter-than-air aviator has for powered machines. It is the story of the sailing-ship and the steamboat over again. The Landervilles may have got a kick out of doing a spot of illegal aviating in their own fashion—just to prove that the modern jet-pilot doesn't yet own the atmosphere." Biggles smiled. "There's no telling what an airman will do when he gets a bee in his bonnet."

THE CASE OF THE
TOO SUCCESSFUL COMPANY

"Good morning, Bigglesworth."

"Morning, sir." Air Detective-Inspector Bigglesworth reached for a cigarette from the box which Air-Commodore Raymond, head of the Air Section at Scotland Yard, pushed towards him.

"What's on your mind?" inquired the Air-Commodore, flicking his lighter.

"Nothing terrific," answered Biggles. "As a matter of fact, things have been so quiet lately that I've had a chance to bring my records up to date. In doing it I came upon an item that strikes me as a trifle odd. It concerns a small charter company, registered in the name of Air Mobility Enterprises Limited. It operates from Gatton Airport."

"What's odd about it?"

"Merely that although it seldom does any business it manages to show a profit."

"How do you know?"

"Because in the first place it continues to carry on when more than one company has had to close down. Obviously it must be doing all right or it would have packed up. Furthermore, Wing-Commander Kellack, the proprietor, apparently makes enough out of it to be able to go to work in a Rolls-Royce."

The Air-Commodore smiled. "Aren't you developing a rather suspicious nature?"

"Surely it's a policeman's job to be suspicious of a thing that doesn't add up to make sense."

"Have you anything against the company?"

"Not a thing. On the contrary, it is most careful to comply with the regulations. Everything is on the top line."

"Then why worry?"

"I'm not worrying. I'm just curious to know how the apparently impossible is achieved. According to its bookings, the company can't possibly pay its way. Its takings would hardly pay the insurance on the two machines it owns."

"Maybe the company is run more efficiently than most of them."

"That's just it. It's *too* efficient. It has never had an accident, never had an argument with the Customs officials or the Air Ministry. In a word, this company is too good to be true."

The Air-Commodore laughed. "That's pretty good. When a company gets slack, you jump on it. When it is run well, you still aren't satisfied."

"I'm bound to be suspicious of a company that doesn't seem to care two hoots whether it gets business or not. This one doesn't even trouble to advertise."

"Yet it gets clients?"

"Occasionally."

"Where do they go?"

"Paris mostly. Sometimes to Le Touquet. Anyway, usually to France. And that raises another point. Why should anyone hire a special machine to go to Paris when British European Airways have machines going there every hour or so?"

The Air-Commodore nodded. "That's true," he said. "What do you suggest doing about it?"

"I want permission to spend a little money. To be precise, I want your authority to book a passage to Paris or Le Touquet by Air Mobility."

"You'll take the trip yourself?"

"No. At this juncture I shall send one of my fellows—probably Ginger. He's quite able to check up that all formalities are properly observed by the machine, passengers and crew."

The Air-Commodore's eyes probed Biggles' face. "What do you suspect—smuggling?"

Biggles shrugged. "I wouldn't say that. But I can't help feeling that there's something phony somewhere. Somehow I don't think it can be orthodox smuggling. The people who run the company must know better than most that you can't keep on diddling the Customs officers and get away with it."

"Who are the directors of the company?"

"One is an ex-wing commander named Oscar Kellack, and the other is a chap named Julius Quick. I've had a look at Kellack's service record. There's nothing wrong with it. I know nothing about Quick. A fellow at the Club told me that at one time he used to run a popular bar in Paris. That may be where Kellack met him, because before he left the service he was there for some time as Assistant Air Attaché. I don't know about that. Anyway, these two run the show with a small staff of mechanics. That's all I know. It is just an idea. If the show turns out to be fair, square and above board, so well and good. We shall do no harm by having a look at it."

"Quite," agreed the Air-Commodore. "Go ahead. Let me know how you get on."

Biggles got up. "If you don't hear any more from me about it you'll know I was barking up the wrong tree."

He went out and returned to his own office.

II

Actually, it was ten days before Biggles' plan could be put into operation. The reason was unusual. When Ginger, acting on Biggles' instruction, and posing as a civilian, rang up the air-line company to book a trip to Le Touquet he was told politely that no bookings could be accepted for the time being because the company's machines were temporarily out of commission for their annual complete overhaul. If, however, he would leave his address he would be informed when the company was again in a position to accept bookings. Ginger gave his private address, and then turned to hear what the others, who were watching, had to say about this unexpected development.

"What do you make of that?" he inquired in a curious voice. "What sort of company is it that manages to have all its machines grounded at the same time?"

"A stinker, old boy, a stinker!" replied Bertie Lissie frankly.

"It's a bit odd, to say the least of it," opined Biggles, tapping a cigarette.

"There's just a chance that it may be more economical to handle both machines together," observed Algy thoughtfully.

"And have to turn down bookings?" exclaimed Ginger. "That doesn't make sense to me. I've got a feeling that Air Mobility don't want genuine clients. They'll never ring me up. You watch it."

"We'll give them a chance," decided Biggles.

Ginger's opinion was shown to be at fault when, a few days later, the company did in fact send him a letter to say that it was now in a position to accept bookings; whereupon he rang up and booked a machine for ten o'clock the following morning.

"A week ago they didn't want customers," he murmured sarcastically. "Now they do. I'd like to know what's happened in the meantime."

"That, my lad, is what you've got to find out," Biggles told him.

And so it came about that ten o'clock the following

c

morning, after the customary formalities—which, incidentally, were observed to the letter—saw Ginger getting into
the seat of a blue-and-silver monoplane. He cast a professional eye over the machine. It appeared to be in a well-
kept condition, but it did not give him the impression of
just having had a complete overhaul. However, that was
only a matter of opinion. He had learned that Wing-
Commander Kellack was to fly the machine.

The pilot and his radio operator came out and took their
places. The aircraft took off, headed south, and put its
passenger down at his continental destination in nice time
for lunch.

Ginger kept a watchful eye on the proceedings, but if
anything unorthodox occurred he did not see it. The only
thing about the trip which, from a professional standpoint,
could be criticised was the height at which the machine
crossed the Channel. It was never more than a few hundred
feet up. This, in Ginger's opinion, considering the single
power-unit with which the machine was fitted, was too low
for safety. Moreover, there seemed to be no reason for it.
It was not as if visibility was poor and the pilot was one
of those who liked to keep an eye on the "carpet". Visibility,
if not exactly good, was at least fair, and Ginger would
have taken the machine up to a much higher altitude before crossing the water. As it was, he was far from comfortable, knowing that engine failure would inevitably land
them in the "drink". The fact that the machine climbed
after crossing the French coast, when altitude was less
important, made the pilot's behaviour even more singular.
But, of course, Wing-Commander Kellack was not to know
that his passenger was also a professional pilot.

Ginger had arranged for the machine to wait for him,
and take him home after he had conducted some imagin-
ary business in the town. What in fact he did was watch
the crew of the aircraft; but nothing they did could be
regarded as in the slightest degree suspicious. They, like

he, had to clear Customs; and there was certainly nothing lax about the way this was done by the French officials.

On the return trip the machine went straight up to five thousand feet and stayed there. This was normal. Why, wondered Ginger, had the pilot not done that on the way out? He returned to Biggles with a slight feeling of frustration, as if he had missed something.

"Well?" queried Biggles.

"Nothing happened," reported Ginger, tossing his cap into a chair. "Not a thing."

Biggles' eyes twinkled. "What you mean is, nothing that you could see."

"I was wide-awake all the time," protested Ginger. "I didn't relax for an instant."

"Maybe," conceded Biggles. "But there, you can't see an awful lot from the inside of an aircraft."

Ginger looked hard at Biggles' face. "What are you getting at?" he demanded. "Are you telling me that something irregular *did* happen?"

"Yes."

"How do you know?"

"I was watching."

Ginger blinked. "*You* were watching?"

"That's what I said. I was waffling along at a comfortable distance behind you."

"You might have told me what you were going to do," complained Ginger indignantly.

"In which case you would have twisted your neck round trying to see me, and Kellack might have wondered what you were goofing at," answered Biggles smoothly. "Kellack's no fool or he wouldn't have been a winco in the R.A.F."

"Okay. And just what did you see?" inquired Ginger, sitting down.

"I saw a small object drop off the machine."

"Where?"

"The moment you crossed the French coast."

"We crossed over that depressing area of sand-dunes just south of Boulogne."

"Quite right. Did you happen to notice a little picnic party there? It consisted of a fellow and a girl. They had what looked like some packets of food spread out on a yellow rug."

"Pah, a courting couple!" snorted Ginger. "We flew right over them."

Biggles nodded. "They looked like a courting couple, I'll admit. That, I suspect, was what they were intended to look like."

"Go on."

"Naturally, I sheered off. Had I stayed too close someone may have thought I was snooping. But it seemed to me that the couple in the dunes must have seen the thing fall off the machine, because they went for a short stroll which took them over the spot and one of them picked the thing up."

"Then what?"

Biggles smiled faintly. "They collected their kit, wandered along to the road, where they had a car waiting, and drove off. It all looked so perfectly innocent. I said *looked*."

"So it's just an ordinary smuggling racket, after all," muttered Ginger.

"Smuggling, certainly, in that Kellack took with him something that he didn't want to declare to Customs. But I'm not so sure that it comes into the ordinary class."

"What do you think Kellack dropped?"

Biggles shrugged. "Your guess is as good as mine."

"I didn't see him drop anything."

"Of course you didn't. With a passenger inside he wouldn't be such a fool as to open a side window and toss something out. Even the most simple-minded passenger would think that was strange behaviour, and possibly report it. The thing seemed to drop off the bottom of the fuselage. It would be the easiest thing in the world for an experienced man like Kellack to fix a little bomb-rack which could be operated from the cockpit. Anyway, the object dropped was a very small one, and for that reason alone I think we've struck something unusual. There are other reasons, too, for thinking that. Why should these people be willing to operate only on special occasions? Ordinary contraband, like gold or currency, could be dropped at any time. Ten days ago Kellack was not willing to fly. Today he is. Why? Obviously, because today he had in his possession something he didn't have ten days ago. That, at least, pretty well proves one thing. Kellack isn't interested in commonplace charter work or he would have booked your flight when you first rang up. That tale about the machine being overhauled was an excuse to put you off."

"So it boils down to this. These Mobility merchants are not what they pretend to be."

"That's the English of it."

"What are you going to do about it?"

"For the moment, exercise a little patience. Kellack has got away with it this time, and there's nothing we can do about today's affair. No doubt this little racket has been going on for some time, in which case, as there must be easy money hanging to it, you can be quite sure that it will continue. Nothing is so dangerous as success. The weakness of the average crook is, he doesn't know when to stop. The next time Air Mobility pull their little trick should be the last. We'll be waiting."

"Where are you going to jump on them—at the airport?"

"No. It would be better to do it over the other side and grab them in the act."

"That'll mean bringing in the French police."

"Why not? It's as much their affair as ours. They'll appreciate our willingness to share the show with them, and do as much for us another day. I'll ring up Marcel

Brissac at the *Sûreté* and we'll set the trap together. It'll be nice to see Marcel again, any way."

"How will you know when Kellack has another little parcel to take over?"

"Now we know what goes on, a little organisation should iron out such minor difficulties," said Biggles. "There's nothing more we can do for the moment."

"Why not?"

"Because the aircraft of Air Mobility Limited are again out of commission."

Ginger's eyebrows went up. "How do you know?"

Biggles grinned. "I don't know. I'm guessing. Let's see if I'm right." He reached for the telephone, put through the call, and inquired about a passage to the Continent on the following day. His smile broadened as he said, "Thank you," and hung up. "Nothing doing," he said, turning back to Ginger. "All machines are booked to capacity for the next few days."

"Do you believe that?"

"Not a word of it. The fact is, Air Mobility are only mobile when they want to be; and that's only when they have a packet to drop on the other side of the Channel. This is getting quite interesting. But let's go and have a cup of tea."

III

A week elapsed, and it was the following Monday before Biggles was able to secure a booking for the Continent on the Wednesday. On this arrangement his plans were made. This time Bertie would be the passenger. His job, apart from providing a reason for the flight, was merely to maintain contact with the machine. Algy was already at Gatton Airport, keeping an eye on things, in the role of an idle spectator. Biggles and Ginger were to go to France, meet Marcel, and take up a position in the sand-dunes to watch

events. Upon what happened there would their own actions
depend. It was there, Biggles thought, that the first arrests
would be made.

On the Tuesday, therefore, Biggles and Ginger flew to
Paris, where Marcel met them and a conference was held.
They spent the evening together. The following morning,
in Marcel's car, they made an early start for the objective
—the desolate sandhills that fringe the French coast in the
region of Boulogne. Biggles had, of course, noted the exact
spot where the charter machine had crossed the coast on
the occasion when Ginger was the passenger. Near this,
some time before the machine was due, they took up a
comfortable position from where they could watch without
being seen.

They had not long to wait before the first move by the
other side was observed. A big car came crawling along
the sea-road as if the occupants were admiring the landscape. It pulled in to the side, and came to a stop some
four or five hundred yards away. A man, and a woman
with a mop of fair hair, got out, the man carrying what
appeared to be a picnic-basket, and the woman, over her
arm, a yellow rug. It was, as Biggles remarked, all perfectly
innocent and natural. The pair might have been holiday-
makers intending to spend the day on the beach. Un-
hurriedly, arm in arm, they strolled into the dunes towards
the sea. About midway between the road and the sea they
looked about as if seeking a comfortable place to sit, and
eventually chose a slight depression between some dunes
which commanded a view of the sea. The place was not
much more than a hundred yards from where the watchers
were now lying flat in the coarse grass that occurred at
intervals.

Here, in the most natural manner possible, the couple
spread the rug. Having disposed themselves on it, they
began to unpack the luncheon-basket. So casual and open
was their behaviour that, as Marcel said, it would have

been a very astute coastguard who saw anything suspicious in their actions. Indeed, so ordinary did the whole thing appear that had it not been for the yellow rug the watchers would have had good reason to think they were making a mistake. But the rug was significant. Ginger perceived that as a marker it would be even more conspicuous from the air than it was from the ground.

Biggles looked at his watch. "If the machine left on time it should be here any minute now," he remarked.

Apparently the machine did leave on time, for almost at once a distant drone announced its approach; and presently it could be seen, flying very low, heading directly towards them.

Thereafter things moved swiftly.

The machine, flying level, raced low overhead, at a height of certainly not more than a hundred feet. As it did so a small object detached itself and hurtled down, to strike the soft sand within a score of paces of the picnic-party. The machine held straight on without deviating a yard from its course.

The picnickers made no great haste to investigate the object that had fallen, although they must have seen it. Not until the aircraft was almost out of earshot did the woman get up, and, after a good look round, stroll in the most casual manner imaginable towards the spot where the object had struck the earth.

Her attitude underwent a quick change, however, when there came a warning shout from her companion, and looking round she saw Biggles, Ginger and Marcel walking briskly towards her. She hesitated for a moment as if in indecision. There may have been something in the manner of those approaching that suggested that they, too, had seen the object fall. At all events, she ran forward, and, being nearer to the object, reached it first. By this time Biggles and his companions were within a dozen yards. Marcel called on the woman to surrender. She snatched up what appeared to be a small canvas bag, and dashed back towards her companion, now on his feet.

Ginger sprinted after her, and was fast overtaking her when a curious thing happened. The woman snatched off her skirt and flung it at him. Ginger caught it, tossed it aside, and went off after his quarry, who, now in a pair of men's shorts, made better time. However, Ginger overtook her and made a grab. It so happened that his hand closed over her hair. It came away in one piece. Then, of course, he perceived the truth. The supposed female was a fake. "She" was, in fact, a man.

If the affair was taking on the character of a comedy, and there was more than a suggestion of it, drama was near. As they raced towards the car the exposed female flung the bag to his companion, and turned in a flash, automatic in hand. Ginger was probably never nearer to death than he was at that moment, for his own gun was in his pocket. He had had no occasion to produce it. The automatic spat twice. The first shot whistled past his face. The second grazed his upper arm, drawing blood. Then there was a shot behind him and his assailant crumpled on the sand. It transpired later that Marcel had fired over Ginger's shoulder.

The second man, holding the bag in his left hand, was now well on his way to the car. And he did in fact reach it first. But before he could get the car going Biggles had run up and put a bullet through the tyre. Seeing that he now had to face three men with guns in their hands, the fugitive must have perceived that further resistance was futile. Anyway, with the fear of death on his face he put his hands up. That was the end of the affair as far as immediate action was concerned.

At Biggles' request Marcel went off and brought his car to a point as near as the ground would permit. The wounded female impersonator, who was obviously in a bad way, was carried to it, and rushed to the hospital at Boulogne, where, it may now be said, he died a week later.

Not until his companion had been lodged in gaol were the contents of the bag examined. Then, in the Police Bureau, Biggles cut the cord that secured the mouth and discharged the contents on the table. There was dead silence for a moment as a cascade of glittering jewels poured out.

Biggles spoke first. "Inspector Hodson, of C. Branch, will be tickled pink when he sees this little lot," he observed grimly.

Marcel requested enlightenment.

"From the published description, these are the jewels of the Countess of Bedlington," said Biggles. "They were stolen from her London house a few days ago. This, apparently, is how they were to be got out of the country. And they're not the first sparklers to come out this way, I'll warrant. For the past twelve months Hodson has been tearing his hair trying to work out how the proceeds of a series of jewel robberies could disappear without trace. As a matter of detail I suggested to him that perhaps they were being flown out, but he was convinced that they were still in the country."

"If the man we've got in gaol will talk, we may be able to find some more," suggested Marcel hopefully.

"Let's try him," agreed Biggles.

"What about the aircraft?" put in Ginger.

"We'll take care of that when it gets back home," answered Biggles.

The captured man turned out to be one of those cosmopolitan spiv types so many of whom make a precarious living by their wits in Paris. His name, real or assumed, was Igor Louensky. Like most of his kidney, now that he was caught he was not only "out", but very much down in the mouth, and ready to blame everyone but himself for what had happened. The popular saying, "honour among thieves", certainly did not apply in his case. Not only was he willing to talk, but he went out of his way to betray all his associates. As a result, the whole gang was soon in the net cast by the French police.

It began in Paris. Louensky had insisted that he did not know what was in the bag—which may or may not have been true. He admitted that he had done similar jobs before, but he was, he declared, just a messenger. His part was to sit on the sands, pick up a bag dropped by an aeroplane, and take it to the bar named the Two Pigeons, in Paris. There he was to hand it over to a man whom he described, known in the Underworld as Harry. He did not know his real name. Everyone knew Harry. Harry was, he thought, the big man of the racket.

Without any difficulty, hoping no doubt to get a lighter sentence, Louensky was persuaded to complete his assignment. That is to say, he went on to Paris and handed over the bag as arranged. The police, in plain clothes, were also there, and Harry was arrested with the goods on him. A search of the luxurious apartment he maintained revealed the proceeds of several jewel raids, not only in Britain but on the Continent.

With the French end "buttoned up" it did not take long to ascertain the part played by Air Mobility, Limited. With Inspector Hodson, Biggles went to Gatton Airport and interviewed the Managing Director, Wing-Commander Kellack, in his office. Seeing that the game was played out, Kellack made a clean breast of everything. He had, he said bitterly, behaved like a fool, an opinion with which Biggles agreed.

It was the old story of bad companions. Air Mobility had started as a genuine air-transportation company, but things had gone badly, and the concern was pretty well on the rocks when, at an unfortunate moment, Kellack had met a man whom he had known just after the war when he was stationed at the French capital. This was Harry.

Harry, then a black-market operator, had cashed a cheque for him at a time when this was unlawful. This act of folly had put him in the man's power, a circumstance which Harry used to his advantage. In a word, under the threat of exposure, Harry had blackmailed the wretched Wing-Commander into working for him. This, of course, was the reason why Air Mobility had been kept on its feet. It must have suited Harry very well, always to have air transport available for his cross-Channel journeys. Kellack was given twelve months' imprisonment to ponder his foolishness.

As Biggles summed it all up in his report to the Air-Commodore, it became clear that Harry, an international rogue, was the evil genius behind more than one racket that had worried the police for a long time. He had made a considerable fortune out of black-market transactions, but when currency regulations were tightened up enough to make this unprofitable he had turned to more direct crime. Somehow he had made contact with the leading jewel-thieves, and relieved them of the difficult business of getting their hauls out of the countries in which they had been stolen. A French court saw to it that he was put where he could do no further mischief for a long time.

Biggles struck the name, Air Mobility Limited, the company that always showed a profit, from his records, with the observation: "Wound up," and the date.

"Give a crook enough petrol," he remarked sadly, "and sooner or later he'll hit the deck."

THE CASE OF THE WHITE LION

"I WANT you, if you will, to run out to West Africa and do a little job for me." As he spoke, Air-Commodore Raymond, head of the Air Section at Scotland Yard, pushed his cigarette-case nearer to his operational chief, Air Detective-Inspector Bigglesworth.

Biggles pulled forward a chair, seated himself and took a cigarette. "What's the worry?" he inquired.

"The worry," answered the Air-Commodore, "is a white lion."

Biggles' expression did not change. "Is that the name of a pub, or club or something?"

"No. I'm talking about a real lion, the well-known tawny-tinted quadruped. Its colour in this case—according to report—is white. That is on the rare occasions when it has been seen in daylight. At night it is said to glow."

Biggles smiled faintly. "Sounds as if someone has been putting in overtime with a case of gin. Cut off the booze and Luminous Leo will disappear with the pink elephants, green snakes, and the more usual members of the alcoholic menagerie."

The Air-Commodore shook his head. "There's more to it than that."

Biggles looked surprised. "You mean, you really believe there is an albino specimen of *felis leo*?"

"I didn't say that, but there could be. After all, white specimens of nearly all animals and birds do occur. There have even been white blackbirds."

"But they didn't glow in the dark," asserted Biggles cynically.

"At all events, whether this beast is there or not, it's causing us a good deal of trouble."

"Is it a man-eater?"

"We've no record of it ever hurting anyone."

"Then what's the fuss about?"

"Africans think nothing of ordinary lions, but they refuse to stay in the locality occupied by a white one."

"We can't blame them for that." Biggles tapped the ash off his cigarette. "You're sure this yarn isn't just native rumour?"

"The white lion has been seen by at least two white men."

"They should have caught it. Any zoo would pay a lot of money for a lion with a milky mane."

"Perhaps they overlooked that possibility." The Air-Commodore smiled whimsically. "I'm offering you a chance. If you can catch the beast you can have it."

Biggles laughed. "Fair enough."

"I want that animal liquidated," averred the Air-Commodore seriously.

"You must have a good reason for that."

"I have. It has cost this country, so far, well over a million pounds. It has also upset the Government's domestic policy to the extent that it may affect this country's supply of meat."

Biggles' eyes opened wide. "Suffering Icarus! How did the brute manage that?"

"I can tell you in a few words," stated the Air-Commodore. "As you know, this country eats more meat than it can produce, therefore we have to spend dollars buying it, or most of it, from South America. Certain people there, knowing that we are dependent on them, have pushed up the price of beef to a figure that we can't afford. Some time ago, therefore, the Government decided it was time we produced our own beef."

"Quite right. I'd turn vegetarian rather than be black-mailed."

"The question was, where to raise the cattle. There are many places in the dominions and colonies where there is almost unlimited grazing, but unfortunately there are snags that make stock-breeding impracticable. Africa is a case in point. The grazing is there, but so are the diseases that kill the type of beef-bullocks we raise in this country. The local cattle, over a period of time, have become immune. If we could introduce that same immunity into our own cattle, all would be well. Scientists got to work, and some time ago they succeeded in producing the animal we required. I must tell you that these experiments, for political reasons, were kept quiet."

Biggles nodded. "Naturally."

"The first area selected for the mass production of our own beef was some extensive plains in the hinterland of Nigeria; a district called Nagoma. A road to it from the coast was put in hand. It was a big job, but according to the programme it was to be ready by the time the first beef was available for shipment. Meanwhile, we put down an airstrip at Nagoma and laid on an airlift. A bungalow was built to accommodate a white manager and three assistants. Stores were flown in, and the calves that were to form the nucleus of the new herd. Native labour was to be employed in rounding up the cattle. As there are several villages in the district we did not think there would be any difficulty about that. Nor was there. Everything was going fine when——"

"The white lion ambled into the picture."

"Exactly. The brute fairly threw a spanner into the gears. Common or garden lions the natives didn't mind, although as a matter of detail they are not common around Nagoma. But the ghastly ghost of one prowling the plains in the small hours was more than they could stand. The whole district promptly evacuated itself of its human population, faster than if the devil himself had appeared on the scene. Nothing will induce the natives to go back. In a word, our scheme collapsed like a punctured football."

"What about the cattle?" queried Biggles.

"They bolted, too. The herd has scattered far and wide."

"Does this mean that the scheme has been abandoned?"

"Certainly not. But it's held up for the time being, and will remain held up until we tear the hide off the unnatural beast to prove to the natives that they have nothing to be afraid of."

Biggles looked puzzled. "Tell me this. Why has nobody shot this brute?"

"It never appears in daylight. That is to say, it has never been seen in daylight by any member of our staff who happened to be carrying a rifle."

"Did your manager try to track the animal?"

"He and his assistants did their best, you may be sure. They hunted day and night, until they were worn out. It seems that this particular beast has an uncanny knack of avoiding trouble. That, of course, to the natives, simply confirms their belief that the creature isn't flesh, blood and hair. Everything has been tried—traps, poison, and the rest—but the lion is still there; and while it is there the scheme will stand still."

Biggles stubbed his cigarette. "Who were the white men who saw the lion?"

"Kirby, our manager, was one. That was early on. He was unarmed at the time."

"It didn't attack him?"

"No. He says he shouted at it and it made off."

"Who was the other man?"

"A fellow named Periera. He's a professional naturalist; collects insects, reptiles and small mammals for natural-history museums. He has his headquarters at some abandoned copper-workings a few miles from our

bungalow. He was on friendly terms with our men. He
joined Kirby in the hunt. Indeed, I gather he was just as
keen as Kirby to bag the beast. No doubt he would have
got a lot of money for the skin. Apart from that, he
complains that he can't get labour now, either. On one
occasion he fired at the lion from such close range that he
says he doesn't know how he missed it. The experience
startled him. He hinted to Kirby that there might be
something in what the natives were saying, after all—that
the beast wasn't natural. This story got out, too, and did
nothing to help matters."

"What nationality is this chap?"

"I don't know; but he isn't British. From his name he
might be Spanish or Portuguese, or even an American of
that ancestry."

"Is he still there?"

"Presumably."

"What about Kirby and his assistants?"

"They've come home to report. There was nothing they
could do there. They say they are faced with an impossible
task. Certainly there's no point in their going back until
the lion is shot, or caught. That's why I suggested that
you might like to go out and have a look at things."

"Why me? I should have thought it was more a job for
a professional big-game hunter."

"I'd like you to have a shot at it first, for several reasons.
In the first place, with aircraft available, you're highly
mobile. Then there is the question of security. The
Government doesn't want this story to get out or we should
be the laughing-stock of the rest of the world. You and
your fellows are experts in operating aircraft on terrain
where there are no servicing facilities. Last, but not least,
you're not likely to be scared by an apparition."

Biggles smiled. "Thank you, sir. Very well. This
promises to be interesting. I've seen most wild beasts, but a
white lion is a new one on me."

"You don't want to speak to Kirby?"

"No. I don't think there is much he can tell us after what you have said. It would be better if no one knew we were on our way."

"As you wish. You can take the docket. You'll find everything in it, from maps of the district to the key of the manager's bungalow. You'll stay there, I imagine. You'll find it comfortable. Everything has been laid on."

Biggles picked up the manila packet that held the particulars of the case. "Expect us back when you see us," he said. "I'll have the hide off this ignoble King of Beasts— or he'll have mine."

II

Four days later an air-police Proctor aircraft was being unloaded on the somewhat overgrown airstrip near to which the manager's bungalow overlooked a typical African landscape. For the most part it comprised a vast expanse of sun-dried grass dotted with smallish, flat-topped trees, standing alone or in little groups. Occasional patches of scrub that had been cut or burnt off were beginning to sprout again. Where the ground fell away into a depression reeds flourished round a pool of stagnant water. Near it, a few head of cattle, apparently the remnants of the herd, were grazing.

The bungalow, raised on piers two or three feet above the ground, was a simple timber-framed building that had been transported in sections to provide temporary accommodation. A verandah ran the whole length of the front. There were some outbuildings in the rear. A hundred yards distant stood a native village, a collection of cone-shaped reed-and-wattle huts built roughly in the form of a circle. A complete absence of life, or smoke, indicated that it was deserted.

The only human beings in sight were the four men unloading the Proctor and carrying the stores and equipment it had brought into the bungalow. They were Biggles himself, with air-constable Ginger Hepplethwaite, Bertie Lissie and Algy Lacey. The equipment included rifles and guns with their appropriate cartridges. When everything was out of the machine Biggles taxied it to the middle of the village, where, as he told the others, it would be out of the way and reasonably safe. This done he returned to the bungalow, where Ginger was boiling water on a Primus-stove for coffee.

"Any sign of the lion?" asked Ginger.

"No," answered Biggles. "I didn't expect to find him waiting for us. Judging from the way those cattle are standing at the pool I don't think he can have been this way lately. He may show up, though, when he sees we're here."

Algy looked up from a case he was opening. "What exactly do you mean by that?"

"Well, now that everyone has been scared away there's no particular reason for the lion to come in this direction, is there?" There was a curious inflection in Biggles' voice.

"Am I to take it from that remark that you really believe in this fantastic beast?" asked Algy.

"Oh, yes. There's a lion here. There was never any doubt in my mind about that," replied Biggles, dropping into the late manager's easy chair. "It wasn't mere hearsay that caused this place to be evacuated. Kirby certainly saw something, and he's prepared to swear it was not only a lion, but a white lion. It must have looked like a lion, anyway. Since it's put him out of a good job he would be the last man to make up such a tale. We're here to find out just what he did see."

"But you don't really think it's a lion?" challenged Ginger.

"I'm keeping an open mind about it," returned Biggles. "It's too late to do anything today. Tomorrow we'll have a look round. Lions have to eat. These imported calves must be easy prey. If there's a lion in the district we may reasonably expect to find where he made a kill. Certainly the larger bones would be left. To my mind, the queerest part of Kirby's story is that neither he nor his assistants ever found a kill. There's something very odd about that."

"The natives saw nothing remarkable in it," averred Ginger. "It supported their arguments that the beast was a ghost, and ghosts, good, honest, respectable ghosts, don't eat."

"All right. It'll be interesting to see how this ghost behaves when he get a four-fifty Express bullet in his ribs."

Bertie stepped in. "But look here, old boy, even if we find a kill it wouldn't follow that the beastly lion that did it was white."

"Admittedly," conceded Biggles. "But it will be something to work on. We've nothing else. If we find a kill we'll watch it. Most beasts of prey return to a kill—if there's anything left over from the previous meal."

The sun was well down by the time the stores had been housed and the bungalow made shipshape. Two rifles and two ten-bore guns, with ammunition beside them, lay ready for action on a side-table. After supper, deck-chairs were taken out on to the verandah, and while watch was kept on the landscape the mission was discussed in all its aspects. As darkness closed in the cattle left the water-hole and walked toward some higher ground. They moved without haste, but with an alert watchfulness, sometimes stopping to gaze fixedly in one direction or another.

"Those beasts are nervous," declared Algy. "They behave as though they know this is the dangerous time. I'd say there are lions about, even if the white one is not on the job."

As if to confirm his words, from out of the misty shadows, a long way off, came the sound that is like no other—the vibrant roar of a lion.

For a few seconds no one spoke. All eyes were turned in the direction from which the sound had come. Then Biggles said: "That naturalist fellow, Periera, lives somewhere over there. That lion can't be far away from him."

"How about walking over and calling on him?" suggested Bertie.

"We'll do that tomorrow," answered Biggles. "There's no particular hurry, and I see no point in wandering about in the dark looking for the place. I'd rather get my bearings in daylight. Which reminds me, I haven't made up the log-books. They're in the machine. I don't want to waste time in the morning, so I'll go and fetch them."

"I'll fetch them for you," offered Ginger.

"Thanks. Take a torch with you."

"You bet I will."

Ginger set off with no more concern than if he had been going on an errand in a city street; but by the time he had reached the silent, deserted *kraal*, he was beginning to look hard at the shadows. It was darker than he had thought. For the first time he began to understand what it would be like to have a white lion prowling about at night. No wonder the natives had departed. He was glad to have his torch. Losing no time he took the log-books from their usual place and hastened back towards the bungalow. As he emerged from the village a curious thing happened. Far away across the lonely plain he saw a spark of light. But even as he stopped and stared at it, it disappeared. He walked on, watching the direction, but it did not reappear. He entered the house somewhat hurriedly.

Biggles was lighting a candle. He looked up, smiling. "What's the matter? Is the lion after you?"

"No, but I saw a light."

Biggles stopped what he was doing. "A light? Where?" Ginger indicated the direction.

"That must be Periera," said Biggles slowly. "No native would be out at night—here, of all places. What's Periera doing, anyway? He's half afraid the lion is really a spook. According to Kirby, his nerve had pretty well gone, and he was talking of moving somewhere else. Why should the light go out, I wonder?"

"It went out as soon as I stepped clear of the village," volunteered Ginger. "It was as if someone was coming this way, but, seeing my light, switched off and turned back."

"I should have thought it was all the more reason for coming on," said Biggles pensively. "I mean, if it was Periera, it hardly looks as if he's nervous, does it? Of course, there's a chance it may have been someone else. No matter. I'm going to turn in. I want to be on the move early in the morning."

III

Some time during the night Ginger woke up. This was so unusual that he thought some sound or movement must have been responsible, although he had no recollection of any such thing. He sat up and looked around. Brilliant moonlight streaming through the open windows revealed the others asleep in their beds. Their easy breathing was the only sound that broke the sullen brooding silence of the African night.

Satisfied that all was well, he turned over to resume his rest; but hardly had he done so than a most singular noise brought him again to the alert. It was as if someone had indulged in a mighty yawn. His nerves tingled, as he listened. It was not repeated. He stared at the window, for it was, he thought, from that direction that the sound had come. Getting out of bed, quietly, so as not to disturb the others, he tiptoed across and looked out.

At the sight that met his gaze he ceased to breathe. It might almost be said that he ceased to live. At any rate, his limbs refused to function. The only sense that remained operative was sight, and even this was not entirely under control. It remained fixed; fixed on an object more frightful than anything a nightmare imagination could have conjured up. Before him, not ten yards away, was the face of a lion. The beast was looking at him. It appeared to be lying down; and as it was facing him he could see no other part of its body. It was no ordinary lion. Reflected moonlight gleamed yellow in unwinking eyes. Around them rippled a weird, blue-white glow.

How long Ginger stood staring at this nerve-shaking spectacle he did not know. It may have been seconds, or minutes. Then it was the lion that broke the spell. There was nothing hostile about its behaviour. It merely opened its mouth wide in a lazy yawn. Then, without any fuss, it got up and walked away, revealing as it did so a grey-white body.

Ginger's reaction would not have qualified him for a decoration. He staggered back into the room, crying incoherently: "Look out! It's here! It's here!" Then he seemed to come to himself, and, remembering the rifles, made a rush for one. Snatching the nearest, he thrust a cartridge into the breach and dashed back to the window, nearly knocking Bertie over on the way for by this time everyone was out of bed, wanting to know what was happening. Biggles switched on a torch. By then, Ginger was leaning out of the window looking for the lion. Not a sign of it could be seen. But he heard a sound in the distance—or he thought he heard a sound—as strange as the one that had brought him out of bed. It was as if someone had blown several short blasts on a whistle. Later, on being questioned, he admitted that he was not quite certain of this because of the noise going on in the room behind him.

Biggles' voice, brittle with annoyance, quelled the tumult. He strode over to Ginger. "What the deuce do you think you're playing at?" he demanded with asperity.

"Playing!" Ginger's voice was shrill with indignation. "I like that! I'm not playing. It was the lion. I saw it."

"Where?"

"Just outside the window. It was there a couple of minutes ago. It was awful."

Biggles looked at him suspiciously. "Are you sure you weren't dreaming?"

"Dreaming, my foot! The thing stood there staring me in the eyes."

"Give me that rifle." Biggles snatched it, opened the door and ran outside. The others, grabbing weapons, followed. There was nothing there. They walked round the bungalow. They stared in every direction, but not a movement could be seen or heard.

"It must have gone," said Ginger lamely.

Biggles led the way back to the bungalow, lit the candle, and requested Ginger, somewhat curtly, to relate exactly what he had seen—or thought he had seen.

Ginger obliged. "Don't let's have any argument about it," he concluded coldly. "It was there all right. I not only saw it; I heard it. And I'll tell you something else," he went on, remembering the last sound he had heard. "There was somebody out there, too. I heard a sort of whistle. It was a long way off, though."

"Zebras," suggested Bertie.

"Nothing of the sort," retorted Ginger. "I've heard a startled zebra whistle. What I heard was nothing like that."

Biggles replaced his rifle on the table. "Okay," he said quietly. "We'll take your word for it that the beast is here. I suppose I should have mounted a guard, but it seemed unnecessary. The last thing I expected was that the lion would come here to call on us. There's nothing we can do until it gets light. Then we shall know the truth of the matter. If a lion was prowling about outside there should be marks——" He broke off, in a tense attitude, listening.

From outside came a sound of madly galloping hoofs.

There was a rush for the door. From the verandah it was possible in the moonlight to see a small herd of cattle tearing across the plain. But the cause of the stampede was not in sight.

"I can't think of anything but a lion that would cause those animals to panic," averred Biggles. "All the same, that isn't to say that the lion was a white one."

"If it was the lion I saw, it was white," declared Ginger obstinately. "And I don't care if I never see it again," he added frostily.

"I don't suppose it'll put in another appearance tonight, so we may as well go back to bed and get some sleep," were Biggles' last words on the matter.

Ginger noticed that he did not, in fact, go back to bed. When he himself fell asleep Biggles was still sitting on the edge of his bed, elbow on his knee, chin in hand, deep in thought. Over him curled a thread of cigarette smoke.

The dawn of a fine day found everyone on the move. An examination of the ground outside the bungalow yielded nothing of interest, except that at the place where Ginger had first seen the lion the grass was pressed flat as if by a heavy body. This, Ginger claimed, confirmed his story. The ground, being hard and dry, showed no footprints— or, at any rate, none that a European could follow. Biggles said little, but Ginger knew from his manner that he had decided on a course of action.

As soon as breakfast was finished, Biggles announced his plan. "I don't think it's the slightest use our walking about on the off-chance of coming upon the lion," he said. "No one has seen the animal properly in daylight, so I don't see why we should expect to. You may ask, why has no one seen the beast; for, after all, lions don't go to ground like rabbits, and here there are no rocks or heavy timber that might provide cover."

"Do you know the answer to that question?" asked Algy.

"No," answered Biggles shortly. "I'm going over to ask this fellow Periera if he does."

"Have you reason to suppose that he might know?" inquired Bertie.

"Someone knows," asserted Biggles meaningly. "As Periera is the only white man within fifty miles of us, we'll try him first."

The others looked at Biggles, sensing something behind the words.

"Are you suggesting that this fellow Periera may know more about this business than he pretends?" asked Algy.

"As I've already said, someone does, and he may be the man. There's something about his behaviour that doesn't ring true."

"But what could he gain by playing up this story of a white lion?" questioned Ginger, mildly astonished.

"Money," answered Biggles. "When I'm asked to investigate a case, I've got into the habit of asking myself: Who stands to make money out of it?"

"But how could he make money——?"

"Wait a minute," interrupted Biggles. "Put it this way. As the Government's stock-raising scheme has failed, I started with the theory that someone may have wanted it to fail. It has failed—so far. Why? Because a lion arrives on the scene. That was bad luck for the promoters of the scheme. Conversely, it was a wonderful stroke of good luck for the people who stood to lose money should the scheme succeed. Anyhow, that's how it struck me at first glance. In my opinion, such good luck was too good to be true. White lions are not exactly common. In short, it seemed to me that there was no luck about it. This white lion business was deliberately engineered. Very well. Who stood to lose money should the scheme succeed? We needn't look far for the answer. Obviously, the stock-breeders on the other side of the Atlantic, whose meat we bought in the past, but whose meat we should no longer buy. I kept an open mind until I got here; but in view of what happened last night I'm no longer in doubt about a lion, a real lion, being here. Ginger saw it. We're asked to believe that such an animal exists in nature, and that it came here at this particular moment by accident. Forget it. I'll stake a month's pay that that lion's phony. The whole thing's phony. That will give you an idea of the lines I'm thinking on. Somebody is pulling a clever trick and he can't be far away. Officially there's only one man in this locality, apart from ourselves. I'm going to call on him. Let's get cracking."

"Are we all going?" asked Ginger.

"Yes. But we won't march in a body to the front door —in case he's the man we're looking for. Algy and Bertie will call on our naturalist neighbour and keep him engaged in conversation while Ginger and I have a look round his back yard. As he lives at an old mine, the buildings may be extensive. All right. Let's go. Bring your guns. We may meet the lion—you never know."

A walk of rather more than an hour brought the objective into view. There was no mistaking it, for conspicuous was a great heap of slag. Near it sprawled several low buildings, and, a short distance away, a small native village of the usual beehive-shaped huts. After studying the place through his binoculars Biggles said everything appeared to be more or less derelict, although that was only to be expected. He could see no one. There was no smoke over the village.

The party now split, Algy and Bertie walking straight on towards the mine, and Biggles, with Ginger, striking off to the right, on a detour through some low-lying ground which Biggles thought would bring them to the rear of the buildings without being seen by anyone there. This hope was fulfilled; but just before the actual buildings were reached some hyenas, slinking away from an object, caused Biggles to alter his course towards it.

The object turned out to be a hide—or the remains of one—and the entrails of an animal, presumably the one to which the hide had belonged. Enough of this remained to show that the unlucky beast had been a calf of the imported breed.

Biggles looked at the mess, then glanced at Ginger.

"Queer that a lion should make a kill so near a building," remarked Ginger.

"Still more queer that it should be able to skin, and cut up its prey, with a knife," returned Biggles dryly. "You can see the knife-marks on the hide. If we hadn't come along, in a few minutes the hyenas would have cleaned all this up. Nothing would have remained to show that a beast had been slaughtered. Mr. Periera has no right to kill British Government stock. Incidentally, he must have a big appetite. Come on."

They walked on, cautiously now, to the nearest buildings. They were of stone, of considerable age, although obviously the work of civilised men. Biggles tried the door they came to and threw a significant look at Ginger when he found it locked. However, the wood was rotten, and he had no difficulty in knocking a hole through it with the butt of his rifle. He looked in through the hole, then stepped back. "Take a look," he told Ginger, in a curious voice.

Ginger looked. There was only one object in the place. It was a large, stoutly-built cage. It was not on wheels, but was made portable by a handle at each corner. There was nothing in it. He stepped back. "Apparently Periera was hoping to catch the lion and take it home with him," he observed.

"If my guess is right, you've got it the wrong way round," murmured Biggles. "That cage was used to bring the lion here."

While Ginger was digesting this illuminating remark they continued on to another building, one in better repair than most. Biggles stopped suddenly, sniffing. "Smell any-thing?" he inquired.

Ginger sniffed. "Yes."

"What?"

"A circus."

"Try again."

"Lion."

"Quite right."

In this case, too, the door was locked, but a small, barred window offered possibilities. While Biggles looked through it Ginger noted that the bars had been set recently, in cement.

"Take a look and see if you recognise anything," invited Biggles, stepping aside.

Ginger looked and nearly went over backwards. Just inside was the animal he had seen from the bungalow window. It was sitting quietly, gazing at him, with a piece of meat between its forepaws. Its face still glowed, but not so brightly as it had in the dark. Its body was chalk-white.

Biggles smiled. "So now we know," he said softly.

Ginger's eyes were wide open. "Then this natura-list——?"

"Naturalist, my foot!" interposed Biggles. "I'd make a small bet that he's a performing-lion exhibitor. Not that the poor old lion in there needs much taming. He's too old to do his own hunting, and has to be fed. That's why there are no kills about. He was probably born in captivity. He's seen so many people in his time that he's as docile as a housecat. Remember how he yawned in your face? Comes for his dinner when he's whistled, like a good dog."

"Then the whole thing is a racket?"

"Of course. I warned you that would be the probable answer. Its object was to scare the daylights out of the native cowboys; and it worked, too."

"But the colour?"

"I imagine there wouldn't be much difficulty in spraying a tame lion with a coat of paint and putting a few dabs of the new luminous ink on its face." Biggles pointed to several splashes of whitewash on the ground near the walls of the building. "This is where the job was done. Let's go in and hear what Mr. Periera has to say about it."

They found the pretended naturalist in animated conversation with Algy and Bertie. He was a dapper little man, with a keen, alert manner. Dark, flashing eyes lit up a swarthy, expressive face. Impressive, well-waxed "handlebar" moustaches decorated his upper lip. He was carelessly dressed and unshaven, but his general attitude was one of easy-going friendliness. His face fell, however, when two more visitors walked in. It fell still farther when Biggles, wasting no time, announced who he was and why he was there.

At first the man was inclined to bluster, but Biggles cut him short. "The game's up, Periera," he said curtly. "I've just had a look at your menagerie. It may save you a lot of trouble if you tell us all about it."

The man threw out his hands, hunching his shoulders. "What do I do wrong?" he asked. "I break no laws. I bring my lion to Africa. Why not? He is so sad to be away from Africa."

"In Africa," said Biggles coldly, "lions are not kept as pets. They're shot. Ginger, go and shoot that one outside."

That did the trick. Periera sprang up in genuine consternation. He seemed to be about to burst into tears. "No! Ah, no!" he cried. "Marco is my only friend. For years he worked for me at the circus. He hurts no one. He do what I say. I put my head in his mouth. He will not bite. He is too old. He has no tooth, no claw."

The man turned pleading eyes on Biggles' face, but he found little sympathy there. He slumped into his chair. "Okay," he said in a resigned voice. "What d'you want to know? I tell."

The story told by the lion-tamer—for that was, in fact, his profession—was much as Biggles had surmised. He was working in South America, he said, when a man unknown to him had offered him a big sum of money to do what he had done. The surprising revelation was that he, Periera, complete with his lion in its cage, had been flown direct to Nagoma. The lion, too old and feeble to do his own hunting, had to be fed. At night, Periera explained, Marco was let loose for exercise, but always returned to be fed at the sound of the whistle. He was never let out in daylight, for fear he might be seen near the mine. There was also a risk of his being shot. That, really, was all there was to it. As Biggles remarked later, it was all very simple.

Periera went on to say that his work was finished long ago. He had been engaged only for a month. Then the aircraft was to come and take him, and his lion, back home. That was three months ago. The plane had not come. His food was finished. He was stranded. He was in despair.

"Those who deal with crooks must expect crooked deals," Biggles told him. "The plane," he declared, "will never come. Why should these people trouble to come and fetch you?" he asked.

Periera stared. Apparently this aspect had not occurred to him.

"You have done the mischief you were sent to do, so you could stay here till Doomsday for all they care," went on Biggles bitingly. "It's lucky for you we came along. I can't take you back to America, of course, but there are people in England who will be interested in your story. Behave yourself and do what you're told and you may not have much to worry about." Biggles turned to Algy. "You and Bertie can take him home. The Air-Commodore can decide what to do with him. I'll stay here with Ginger for a bit."

"But Marco," pleaded Periera. "He will die. He must eat."

"I'll take care of him," answered Biggles. "He has done the mischief. Only he can undo it. You put him in his cage and maybe arrangements can be made for you to fetch him later. Meanwhile, we'll send word round the district to let the natives know that the White Lion of Nagoma is on view—behind bars. That should bring them back."

Half an hour later, as Algy and Bertie marched off with their prisoner towards the bungalow, Biggles remarked to Ginger: "I agree with Periera; it seems a shame to bump off poor old Marco. After all, it wasn't his fault. He must hate his coat of paint as much as anybody. No doubt it will wear off in time. He's probably a gentleman compared with some members of the human species. What will they think of next?"

THE CASE OF
THE REMARKABLE PERFUME

As BIGGLES entered the office of his chief at Scotland Yard, Air-Commodore Raymond of the Air Section, his eyes rested for a moment on a small, lean, tired-looking little man who sat in the visitor's chair. He noticed that his skin was of that curious pallor, a sort of neutral tint, that is so often the result of living in an unhealthy part of the tropics. An old felt hat rested on his knees.

"Oh, Bigglesworth, this is Mr. Eustace Cotter," introduced the Air-Commodore. "He was sent here by the Colonial Office. He's in a spot of trouble. I'd like you to hear his story. We could then decide if it is possible for us to help him."

Biggles pulled up a chair, accepted a cigarette, and lit it. "Go ahead, Mr. Cotter," he invited. "I'm listening."

The visitor cleared his throat. "I am, in the way of business, an explorer—or, if you prefer the word, a prospector," he began. "That does not mean, however, that I am concerned only with gold or precious stones. The modern professional prospector has a wide range of commodities to seek, from base metal deposits to the plants and herbs from which many patent medicines are derived. It would be true to say that today everything has a commercial value. The only questions are the quantities in which the commodity exists and the transportation facilities available. For my own part I have specialised in the aromatic oils and gums from which most perfumes

D

are derived—for which purpose, I should tell you, I am
financed by the well-known firm of Goray. Perfume is a
bigger business than is generally supposed, for it is used
for a hundred purposes besides the common ones of scent,
cosmetics, and toilet preparations. Every woman, and
nearly every man, uses perfume in one form or another
every day. You use it in your shaving-soap and your hair-
cream. In short, we live in days when everything has to
have a pleasant smell, and consequently the creation and
production of basic aromas employ an enormous number of
people. A good perfume, or better still, a *new* perfume,
can be worth millions to the economy of a country that
must export its goods, as we must, to buy food. I'm sorry
to have to go into this, but it is necessary that you should
understand that perfumery is not just a luxury trade. It
is big business."

Biggles nodded. "I follow."

Mr. Cotter continued. "Now let us get on. Nearly all
good perfumes are obtained from a vegetable base, from
the essential oil extracted from flowers, leaves, the bark of
trees, roots, and even the seeds of plants. Vanilla, for
example, so popular as a flavouring, is derived from the
seed-pod of a climbing variety of tropical orchid. The word
itself is Spanish, meaning a little scabbard, because that
is the shape of the seed-pod."

Biggles smiled. "I'll remember it every time I eat an
ice-cream," he promised.

"I will now come to the point," went on the explorer.
From his pocket he took a wallet. From this he selected
an envelope, which yielded a piece of stiff white paper,
folded once. This he opened to display what it contained.
It was a small, insignificant flower, pale-blue in colour. A
tinge of excitement crept into his voice as he inquired:
"You don't know what that is?"

"It looks to me like a flower," said Biggles simply.

"It is an orchid."

"Okay," agreed Biggles, without emotion. "If you say so, it's an orchid. I'm no gardener."

"You may have difficulty in believing it," said Mr. Cotter seriously, "but that flower is one day going to cause a sensation. It is worth to the country that first produces it on a commercial scale, at a conservative estimate, twenty million pounds."

"And how much do you, personally, get out of that?" inquired Biggles dryly.

"Something, naturally, I hope," admitted Mr. Cotter frankly. "Why, otherwise, should I risk my life looking for such things? But I shall not get as much as you may think." A note of bitterness crept into his voice. "It is not the explorer, the man who usually dies on his job, who makes the money. It is the people who exploit what he discovers. But every explorer knows that from the outset, so he has really no cause for complaint. Now watch." Mr. Cotter returned the wallet to his pocket and produced a small, screw-topped phial. "This is the seed-pod of the flower I showed you," he said, unscrewing the lid and tipping three or four small brown objects into the palm of his hand.

Instantly the room was flooded with the most wonderful fragrance.

"Did you ever smell anything like that?" cried the explorer enthusiastically.

Even Biggles was impressed. "Never," he admitted.

The explorer returned the phial to his pocket. "The firm that is first in the market with that perfume will take the lead over every competitor," he asserted earnestly. "Every woman will want it."

"I imagine there is some difficulty about collecting this particular posy or you'd have had it in the bag by now?" murmured Biggles shrewdly.

"Quite right," admitted the prospector. "That plant grows in the heart of the South American jungle—to be specific, in the hinterland of British Guiana. Knowledge of it came to me first through native rumour. I spent two years of my life, and nearly ruined my health, finding it. It is the sort of thing every commercial explorer dreams of finding, but seldom does. Unfortunately, I located the plant at the wrong time of the year. The seeds were not ripe. Had they been, I could have brought them home and cultivated the flower under glass. In that way, I could at least have raised enough plants to establish my claim to the perfume. As it was, I was too ill to wait for the seeds to ripen. I collected a few roots, but they died before I could get them to civilisation. Now for the tragedy. I employed native bearers, of course. In charge of them was a half-caste named Ramon. I didn't like the fellow from the start. Too late I realised that he knew more than he pretended and really joined my party for his own ends. He understood the value of what I had found, and deserted me as soon as we were within reach of civilisation. It has now come to my knowledge that he has approached a foreign firm, who have financed him to go back and collect seeds of my botanical treasure. What tale he has told them I don't know; not the true one, I imagine. However, there it is."

"I see," said Biggles slowly. "But this is British territory. Can't the authorities there stop him?"

"No. At least, I think it is very unlikely. The fellow knows the country too well. There would be no need for him to enter through Georgetown, the capital. He could get to the place via Brazil, or French or Dutch Guiana. The only way to beat him is to race him to the spot. No doubt he will travel in the orthodox way, overland, either through the jungle itself or by canoe on one of the several rivers."

"Ah!" murmured Biggles. "I get it. Your idea is to fly there and beat him to it?"

"Exactly."

The Air-Commodore stepped into the conversation. Looking at Biggles, he said: "There is no doubt that Mr. Cotter has a commercial proposition of considerable importance to our export market. Both the Colonial Office and the Board of Trade have agreed on that. But they can do nothing about it. So they passed him on to us, presumably because, as we are the only Government department outside the R.A.F. with aircraft, we might be able to help."

"It's hardly a police job," observed Biggles doubtfully.

"At a stretch it could be made one, I think," answered the Air-Commodore. "After all, this fellow Ramon was employed by Mr. Cotter. He broke his contract. The treacherous scoundrel has stolen something, and has sold it. In my opinion, stealing the fruits of the expedition makes him just as much a thief as if he had made off with a piece of equipment—a rifle or a canoe. And British Guiana is, after all, our territory. Ramon does not hold a Government licence to explore for profit, so he's breaking the law anyway."

"I agree, if you put it like that," answered Biggles. "For moral reasons alone the rascal shouldn't be allowed to get away with it. I'm all against rogues prospering."

The Air-Commodore smiled. "From which I take it that you're prepared to make a trip to British Guiana?"

Biggles shrugged. "I can't say that flower-hunting is in my line, but if it will do any good I'll have a go at it. Is Mr. Cotter prepared to come with us and show us the spot?"

The explorer answered for himself. "Certainly," he agreed with alacrity.

"Fair enough," continued Biggles. "In that case we'd better get to work right away on the practical side of the show." He looked at the explorer. "I take it there is a place handy where an aircraft can be put on the ground?"

"Not on dry ground, I'm afraid. But there is a lake. In

fact, there is a string of lakes, much of the area being low-lying ground that drains mountain systems on either side."

The Air-Commodore got up. "Now that the project has been decided I think you'd better take Mr. Cotter up to your office," he suggested. "You can take your time, there. No doubt he will give you all the information you need."

"Good enough," agreed Biggles. "Come along, Mr. Cotter. The sooner we're airborne the better."

II

Three days later a twin-engined "Scud" amphibian of the Police Flight made a landfall at Natal, in Brazil, having crossed the Atlantic on the regular track from Dakar, in West Africa. In it were Biggles, Algy, Bertie, Ginger and Mr. Cotter. After the usual formalities, and a meal, during which time the aircraft was refuelled, Biggles headed north, and late in the afternoon touched down on the airport at Georgetown, capital of the British colony of British Guiana.

Mr. Cotter's knowledge of the colony was now shown to advantage, and he was able to smooth out the inevitable minor difficulties, such as the importation of firearms. Ramon, he thought, should they meet him, would have native porters, and as these would probably be of a type similar to himself, trouble might be expected.

Having parked their kit at the hotel where the party intended to stay the night, Mr. Cotter went off to make discreet inquiries about the traitorous halfbreed. He re-turned at sundown to report that he could get no news of him, from which it could be assumed that the man was keeping clear of the capital. There was good reason to hope, said the explorer cheerfully, that they were ahead of his renegade employee.

Shortly after dawn the following morning, the Scud took off on the last leg of its journey to the objective, a matter of two hundred miles. Mr. Cotter now shared the cockpit with Biggles. An open map lay on his knees, although, as he said, the weather being fine and visibility good, he did not really need it; for they would for the most part have a dominant landmark in the broad Essequibo River, which, once the coastal region had been crossed, wound a sinuous course through the almost untrodden jungle that rolled westward to the horizon.

Biggles was content to be within reach of the river. To make an emergency landing on it would be a perilous operation, but there would, at least, be a chance of survival. Elsewhere, there would be no chance at all.

After a flight of rather less than two hours the explorer announced that one of several lakes that could be seen ahead was their destination. On the previous occasion that he had been there, he remarked with a smile, the journey had occupied him for the best part of two months. As they approached, he indicated the stretch of water on which he wished to land. Near by, in the surrounding jungle, grew the perfumed floral treasure. A game-track, he said, led to the more or less open savannah where the orchid flourished. The jungle itself was for all practical purposes impenetrable.

In answer to a question from Biggles he said that, as far as he knew, there were no obstructions on the water likely to damage the aircraft in landing. Biggles was afraid of floating logs. Cotter put his mind at rest by asserting that most of the trees of the forest were of wood so hard that they would sink if they fell into the water.

Biggles eyed with misgivings several large colonies of wading birds that occupied the shallows, notably some sort of scarlet crane, or heron. These did, in fact, rise in a spectacular cloud as the aircraft glided in; but by turning away Biggles avoided them without difficulty and continued to lose height. After a trial run he went in to a smooth landing. He went on slowly, watching the water closely, and presently brought the machine to a mooring a few yards from the bank, between some growths of a magnificent water-lily with leaves five feet across. He switched off and looked around. A sultry silence fell. The only sound was the occasional discordant cries from the brightly plumaged birds as they returned to their feeding-ground.

"Wonderful!" exclaimed Mr. Cotter. "This flying certainly makes travel easy over this sort of country. I can't imagine why I didn't think of it before."

"It's all right if you know where you're going, and what you're looking for," answered Biggles. "But I'm afraid you'd find it a bit expensive to cruise around on the off-chance of picking up something worth while."

He joined the others in the cabin, where a picnic lunch had been laid out. As soon as it was finished Mr. Cotter announced his intention of completing his quest forthwith. He was flushed with excitement, and all agog to secure his prize; and as he said he knew just where it was, there appeared to be no difficulty about this. He expected to be away only about an hour; whereupon Biggles said that in that case, as they had ample daylight, they might as well go straight back to the coast afterwards. Although he had come prepared to stay for a day or two if necessary, there was no point in hanging about once the seeds of the orchids had been gathered.

Shortly afterwards, therefore, Mr. Cotter, with a haversack slung over his shoulder, waded ashore. Ginger decided to go with him, both as a matter of interest and also to stretch his legs. He picked up a rifle, not so much because he expected that he would need it, as for the feeling of security it gave.

Actually, having been in a tropical jungle on several occasions, in the walk that followed he saw nothing to excite his curiosity. One jungle, he was aware, is much the same as another. All are uncomfortable places. However, when, following the narrow game-track to which he had referred, Mr. Cotter led the way out of the heavy timber to some open country, this promised to be less uncomfortable than some. There were plenty of orchids of the common sort, but with these the explorer was not concerned. As they walked on he remarked: "It was unfortunate that Ramon happened to be with me on the last occasion that I used this path, otherwise he would not have known the exact habitat of the orchid. Usually, he stayed in camp, being lazy by nature. The crafty rascal must have had a shrewd idea that the orchid was about here. He knew what I was looking for, of course. Indeed, I made no secret of it."

Suddenly the explorer stopped, a hand raised. "Smell," he requested, with a gleam in his eyes.

Ginger caught a whiff of exotic fragrance. "Very nice," he agreed, without, however, sharing his companion's enthusiasm.

Mr. Cotter strode forward. "Here we are!" he exclaimed, and unslinging his haversack started plucking at the plants with the glee of a schoolboy picking ripe apples.

Ginger looked at the orchids, but finding them almost insignificant compared with most of their kind, soon lost interest, and making his way to a dry spot sat down to wait. They were, he reckoned, within a mile of the aircraft, so no possibility of danger entered his mind. The explorer had said that as far as he knew there were no natives in that particular district, probably on account of the hordes of mosquitoes that arose from the margins of the lakes at nightfall. Still, Ginger kept his eyes open; but all he saw to engage his attention for the next half-hour was a snake, which might or might not have been poisonous. He gave it the benefit of the doubt—not that it made any move to molest him.

Mr. Cotter, smiling and triumphant, with a full bag of the aromatic seeds, had just announced that he was ready to return when, from the direction of the lakes, came the hum of an aircraft engine. It persisted for perhaps a minute and then cut out. Ginger paid little attention to it, merely remarking that he hoped everything was all right and commenting on the way the trees muffled the sound, giving the engine a curious note.

Mr. Cotter, shouldering his bag, said casually that Biggles was perhaps moving the aircraft to a better mooring, out of the full glare of the sun—a reasonable suggestion. Nothing more was said, and presently they started on the return journey, well satisfied with the outcome of their quest.

They had covered about half the distance when, rounding a tangle of undergrowth, they came suddenly face to face with two men, one white and the other brown, who were striding along the track. The surprise was mutual. Both parties pulled up short and regarded each other from a distance of ten yards. To Ginger's subsequent mortification he did not grasp the situation as quickly as he thought he should have done. Moreover, he reprimanded himself bitterly for having lazily slung his rifle instead of carrying it in a position in which it might have been of use. The fact remains, he had still not moved when he found himself staring stupidly into the muzzles of two revolvers.

As soon as the man opposite to him spoke, he realised who he was, and what had happened. The noise of the aircraft engine was also explained. The man was Ramon, and he had chosen the same method of transportation as themselves. There was, he saw too late, every reason why he should.

Ramon seemed very amused. "Well, say, boss, ain't that just swell? I guess you've done the job for us," he sneered, in a voice coarse with an exaggerated American accent.

Ginger breathed hard in tight-lipped anger; but there was nothing he could do, perceiving that there was nothing to prevent the half-caste from shooting them down with impunity on the slightest provocation, for the chances of their bodies being found were slight. He had a feeling that had the half-caste not been so sure of himself he would probably have shot them anyway.

Grinning, Ramon stepped forward, relieved Mr. Cotter of his bag and Ginger of his rifle, and returned to his companion. Then his eyes narrowed menacingly. "You two guys will be wise to stay right here for a while," he said coldly. "Come on, Joe. What are we waiting for?"

Laughing, revolvers still in their hands, the two men turned about and strode off back the way they had come.

Ginger nearly choked, and but for the fact that Mr. Cotter laid a restraining hand on his arm he might have acted foolishly. As it was, he could only look at his companion with a mixed expression of chagrin and apology. "I ought to be kicked from one end of America to another," he muttered.

"Why?" inquired Mr. Cotter. "We couldn't have foreseen this."

"In the first place I should have known that the machine we heard wasn't ours," answered Ginger. "Secondly, I should have carried my rifle in my hand instead of hanging it round my neck like a fool."

Mr. Cotter shook his head. "Perhaps it was a good thing you weren't carrying the rifle," he said quietly. "Ramon is a dead shot with that revolver of his. I don't know about the white man. I presume that was the pilot who flew him here."

Ginger was thinking fast now that the effects of shock were wearing off. It struck him that Ramon must have assumed that they were alone in the jungle, or had with them only native porters. At all events, it seemed certain that he had not seen Biggles and his aircraft, or he would not have behaved with such carefree confidence.

"Let's get back to Biggles and tell him what has happened," he said tersely. "We may still be able to knock that crook off his perch." Without waiting for a reply, he set off at his best pace.

Nothing more was said. Ten minutes later, dripping with perspiration, they met Bertie coming towards them. He carried a haversack, and a rifle at the ready.

Ginger, in his exasperation, did not waste time in futile greetings, but at once rapped out the story of their disaster.

Bertie did not seem in the least surprised. "Relax, laddie, relax!" he requested. "Biggles thought something like that might happen, and asked me to toddle along to offer the jolly old helping hand—if you see what I mean."

"Then you saw the other machine arrive?"

"We couldn't help seeing it, old boy. It's down on the next lake."

"Well, it's too late to do anything about it," said Ginger miserably. "That infernal crook Ramon has got the seeds."

"All of them?"

"All those we picked."

"Then let's go back and pick some more."

"And while we're picking them Ramon will be away with a bagful," returned Ginger with biting sarcasm.

"Too bad, laddie, too bad. But Biggles says we're not to come back without the goods."

Ginger hesitated.

"Orders is orders," said Bertie. "Let's go gathering nuts in May."

"We might as well get some while we're here," put in Mr. Cotter.

Ginger shrugged. "Okay," he agreed. "But I should have thought the best plan was to go after Ramon and make him cough up the seeds he took from us. We might just have been in time. However, if that's how Biggles wants it. . . ."

They went back to the area in which the orchids seemed to thrive, and, by all joining in the work, soon filled not only Bertie's haversack but their pockets as well. Bertie agreed warmly with all that Mr. Cotter had said about the peculiar property of the seeds. "Unless we can get this fug out of our togs people will think we're running a bally beauty parlour," he remarked, as they set off for the lake.

Ginger, in his impatience, strode on, expecting every moment to hear Ramon's machine take off.

Reaching the Scud, he found Biggles and Algy having a cup of tea as if nothing out of the ordinary had happened.

"Got the stuff?" inquired Biggles, looking up. "But I needn't ask," he went on quickly. "I can smell it from here. You stink as if you'd been swimming in eau-de-Cologne."

"We've got the stuff all right," answered Ginger. "So has that rat Ramon," he added grimly. He described briefly what had happened. "Instead of sitting here having a tea-party, what's wrong with going after him?" he concluded belligerently. "Maybe we can still race him to the coast."

"No hurry," returned Biggles calmly, breaking a biscuit.

Ginger frowned. "Is Ramon's machine still on the water?"

"Yes."

"Are you sure?"

"Quite sure."

"Then what's he doing? I should have thought he would have been away by now."

"He's probably having a little trouble getting started," averred Biggles casually.

Algy was grinning.

Ginger's eyes narrowed. "What goes on?" he demanded suspiciously.

Biggles answered. "If you were careless, so was Ramon. If we didn't expect him, he didn't expect us. We saw his machine come in, of course, and guessed who it was. We cocked an eye over the rushes and made out that there were only two of them—pilot and passenger. They both went off. That was silly. They made the mistake of supposing they had the place to themselves. The pilot should have stood by his machine. As he did not, naturally we strolled over to have a look at it."

"Then what?"

Biggles' lips twitched. "Nothing much. Merely as a precaution, in case they got into mischief, Algy and I removed the sparking-plugs from the engine as the simplest way of keeping the aircraft on the floor. That, no doubt, is why it is still here."

There was a titter of laughter, induced as much as anything by the expression on Ginger's face.

"What are you going to do about the plugs?" Ginger wanted to know.

"That will depend upon what Mr. Cotter has to say about it," returned Biggles. He turned to the explorer. "Could this unpleasant fellow, Ramon, get back to the coast without an aircraft, do you think?"

"Oh yes," was the reply. "He's an experienced jungle traveller."

"How long will it take him?"

"Not less than six weeks."

"That, I imagine, would give you time to register the new perfume and to put it on the market?"

"Ample time."

"That's capital. Mr. Ramon and his crooked pal can walk home. But come on. By this time they will have discovered why their engine won't start, and they're liable to be peeved about it. As they have firearms it might be a good thing if we moved off before they can use them. I believe in avoiding trouble if it's possible. They'll hear us start up. If they're any good at guessing it won't take them long to work out what's happened to their plugs."

"When they get back they'll kick up a row about you leaving them stranded," predicted Ginger. "They'll lose their aircraft."

"In the ordinary way, I wouldn't think of doing such a thing," asserted Biggles. "But they started the rough stuff, not us. We've a perfectly sound argument in saying that we acted in self-defence. After all, they pinched your rifle. They held you up at the point of a pistol. These are criminal offences. In my view, in those circumstances we are justified in taking steps to prevent them from doing any further mischief; and I'm sure any court would agree. What we've done, in effect, is to sentence them to six weeks' hard labour. They'd get worse than that if we handed them over to the police. But that's enough talking. All aboard. Let's get home."

Everyone took his place in the machine. Ginger sat in the second-pilot's seat. Biggles started up and taxied out to the middle of the lake. As he turned into position for the take-off two men rushed into the shallows, waving frantically.

"Save your strength, you rascals," Biggles told them. "You'll need it."

A few minutes later the machine was in the air, climbing for height as it turned towards the east. On all sides, jungle-matted hills rolled away to the pitiless horizons.

"Fancy having to walk home through that little lot," muttered Ginger.

Biggles laughed.

"Is there something funny about it?" inquired Ginger.

"I think so," answered Biggles. "Ramon and his partner came here to pinch a perfume. Well, they've got it, and no doubt they'll try to hang on to it. But I'll wager that long before they get home everything they've got will so reek of the stuff that they'll wish they'd never seen it. Did you ever hear of poetic justice?"

"Yes."

"Well, you can call this perfumed justice."

Biggles hummed softly to himself as he set a course for the coast.

BIGGLES, THEN AND NOW

THE stories that follow are reprinted to comply with many requests for information about Biggles' early days as an air pilot. They are taken from the first Biggles book published, *The Camels Are Coming*. This and *Biggles of the Camel Squadron* have long been out of print, and copies are rare. Both consist of short stories and deal with Biggles' exploits in the first world war. Biggles was then a junior officer in the Royal Flying Corps, then a branch of the army, for the R.A.F. did not come into existence until 1918. When the books were written the threat of a second world war had not darkened the horizon, and their main purpose was to keep alive the traditions established by the pioneers of war-flying.

Air combat was then very different from what it has become; but let it be remembered that it was in the first world war that the primary lessons of air warfare were learned. Equipment (Biggles flew a Sopwith Camel) was primitive, but bullets struck just as hard as in Hitler's war. "Flak", then called "archie", was just as much a menace, for machines were comparatively slow, had a low ceiling, and were therefore easier to hit than their modern counterparts. There were no parachutes to give pilot or gunner a chance if things went wrong.

In fact, there was none of those things that make the cockpit of a modern aircraft look like a watch-maker's shop. There was no wireless telephony. Once the wheels of an aircraft were off the ground the pilot was his own master, to go where he wished. There was no "blind-flying" equip-

ment, no oxygen apparatus and no electrically heated cloth-
ing. Most machines were fitted simply with an airspeed
indicator, an altimeter, an air engine rev. counter, and an
inclinometer that might as well have been left at home
for all the practical use it was. There might be petrol and
oil gauges, but it was unwise to rely on them. A pilot flew
"by the seat of his pants", with his head in the open air.
One could usually recognise a "Camel" pilot by the oil-
soaked shoulders of his tunic. (The castor-oil used by rotary
engines was thrown out as fast as it was used, and a pilot,
leaning out to see where he was going, collected some of
it on his person.)

True, in 1918 there appeared a machine with a covered
cockpit—the S.E.5. It was promptly dubbed "the green-
house", and at the front the cover was usually removed.
Pilots hated the unaccustomed shut-in feeling.

The Sopwith Camel was an efficient machine in its day,
but tricky to fly. It had little inherent stability. The ex-
cessive "torque" of the rotary engine tended to turn the
whole machine over, and holding on controls to counteract
this was a tiring business. The same torque enabled a
pilot to turn in a flash in one direction, but against torque
the aircraft had to be dragged round.

In short, war-flying in the period covered by these stories
was a simple but dangerous occupation. You took off,
found an opponent, and shot at each other until one
fell, or ran out of bullets. This was air combat in its
infancy, but it lent itself to tricks that could be employed
to advantage. Few pilots lived long enough to become
senior officers, for which reason the average age of a major
commanding a squadron was about twenty-one. We used
to say that if a pilot, after being posted to a service
squadron, could survive the first forty-eight hours he
might live for a month. By that time, if he had learned
the tricks of the trade, he had a reasonable prospect of
life.

The following stories were the first "Biggles" stories ever written. Biggles was a young man then, so if you notice a difference in his behaviour, or if his methods and equipment seem strange, you will understand why.

W.E.J.

THE WHITE FOKKER

To THE casual observer, the attitude of the little group of
pilots clustered around the entrance of "B" Flight hangar
was one of complete nonchalance. MacLaren, still wearing
the tartans and glengarry of his regiment, a captain's stars
on his sleeve, squatted uncomfortably on an upturned
chock. To a student of detail the steady spiral of smoke
from the quickly drawn cigarette, lighted before the last
half was consumed, gave the lie to his bored expression.
Quinan, his "maternity" tunic flapping open at the throat,
hands thrust deep into the pockets of his slacks, leaning
carelessly against the flimsy structure of the temporary
hangar, gnawed the end of a dead match with slow deliberation. Swayne, bareheaded, the left shoulder of his
tunic as black as ink with burnt castor-oil, seated on an
empty oil drum, was nervously plucking tufts of wool from
the tops of his sheepskin boots. Bigglesworth, popularly
known as "Biggles", a slight, fair-haired, good-looking lad
still in his 'teens, but an acting Flight-Commander, was
talking, not of wine or women, as novelists would have us
believe, but of a new fusee spring for a Vickers gun which
would speed it up another hundred rounds a minute.

His deep-set hazel eyes were never still and held a glint
of yellow fire that somehow seemed out of place in a pale
face upon which the strain of war, and sight of sudden
death, had already graven little lines. His hands, small
and delicate as a girl's, fidgeted continually with the tunic
fastening at his throat. He had killed a man not six hours
before. He had killed six men during the past month—or

was it a year?—he had forgotten. Time had become curiously telescoped lately. What did it matter, anyway? He knew he had to die some time and had long ago ceased to worry about it. His careless attitude suggested complete indifference, but the irritating little falsetto laugh which continually punctuated his tale betrayed the frayed condition of his nerves.

From the dim depths of the hangar half-a-dozen tousled-headed ack-emmas watched their officers furtively as they pretended to work on a war-scarred Camel. One habit all ranks had in common: every few seconds their eyes would study the western horizon long and anxiously. A visiting pilot would have known at once that the evening patrol was overdue. As a matter of fact, it should have been in ten minutes before.

"Here they come!" The words were sufficient to cause all further pretence to be abandoned; officers and men together were on their feet peering with hand-shaded eyes towards the setting sun, whence came the rhythmic purr of rotary engines, still far away. Three specks became visible against the purple glow; a scarcely audible sigh was the only indication of the nervous tension that the appearance of the three machines had broken. The door of the Squadron office opened and Major Mullen, the C.O., came out. He would not have admitted that he too had shared the common anxiety, but he fell in line with the watchers on the tarmac to await the arrival of the overdue machines.

The three Camels were barely half a mile away, at not more than 1,000 feet, when a new note became audible above the steady roar of the engines. It was the shrill scream of wind-torn wings and wires. *Whoof! Whoof! Whoof!* Three white puffs of smoke appeared high above the now gliding Camels. *Bang!—Whoof! Bang!—Whoof!* —the archie battery at the far end of the aerodrome took up the story. Not a man of the waiting group moved, but every eye shifted to a gleaming speck which had detached itself from the dark-blue vault above. A white-painted Fokker D.VII was coming down like a meteor behind the rearmost Camel. There was a glittering streak of tracer. The Camel staggered for a moment and then plunged straight to earth. At the rattle of guns the other two Camels opened their engines and half-rolled convulsively. The leader, first out, was round like a streak at the Fokker, which, pulling out of its dive, had shot up to 3,000 feet in one tremendous zoom, turned, and was streaking for the line. The stricken Camel hit the ground just inside the aerodrome; a sheet of flame leapt skywards.

From first to last the whole incident had occupied perhaps three seconds, during which time none of the spell-bound spectators on the tarmac had either moved or spoken. The C.O. recovered himself first, and with a bitter curse raced towards the Lewis gun mounted outside his office. Half-way he changed his mind and swung towards the blazing Camel in the wake of the ambulance, only to stop dead, throw up his hands with a despairing gesture, and turn again towards the hangar.

"Get out, you fool; where do you think you're going—he's home by now," he snapped at Bigglesworth, who was feverishly clambering, cap-and-goggles-less, into a Camel.

As the two surviving Camels taxied in, a babble of voices broke loose. Mahoney, who had led the flight, leaned swaying for a moment against the fuselage of his machine. His lips moved, but no sound came; he seemed to be making a tremendous effort to pull himself together. His eyes roved round the aerodrome to identify the pilot of the other Camel. Manley, half-falling out of the cockpit of the other machine, hurried towards him. "All right, old lad, take it easy; it wasn't your fault," he said quickly.

Mahoney's lips continued to move as he struggled to speak. "It was Norman—poor little beggar! First time over, too—the swine—he didn't give him a chance—not a——" His voice rose to a shrill crescendo.

"Stop that!" cut in the C.O. quickly, and then more quietly, "Steady, Mahoney."

For a moment the Flight-Commander and his Commanding Officer eyed each other grimly. Mahoney's eyes fell first. Slowly he took off his sidcot suit and threw it on the ground with studied deliberation. Cap and goggles followed, leaving that part of his face which they had protected like a white mask.

"Officers in the Orderly Room, please," said the C.O. turning on his heel.

Mahoney lit a cigarette and followed the little group moving towards the Squadron office.

"Sit down, everybody," began Major Mullen. "A bad show. I blame no one. Anybody could have been caught the same way. It might have been me, or it might have been you, Mahoney. From some points of view it was a low-down trick; from others, well, it was a smart piece of work; anyway, the fellow was within his rights. He'd done it before, farther north; I've heard about it. He did it three times at 197 Squadron, once as they were taking off. He'll try again, and if he pulls it off again here it's our own funeral. We've had our lesson. We'll get him; we've *got* to get him. You know the unwritten law about having an officer shot down on his own aerodrome? We can't show our faces in another mess until we *do* get him. You know what Wing will say about this. That's all. Go and get a drink, Mahoney. I'll see Flight-Commanders here in half an hour."

An hour later Major Mullen was running over the result of the conference. "I think Mahoney's right," he said. "The Fokker probably came over the line at eighteen or twenty thousand with his engine off. He must have been watching you all the time, Mahoney. He knew that you were at the end of the patrol and hadn't enough juice left to go back after him. All right, then. Mahoney, you'll take the patrol in the morning; come back in the ordinary way when it's over. Bigglesworth, you'll take your Flight to the ceiling. Hang around over Mossyface Wood until you see Mahoney coming back and then follow him home. Stay as high as you can and don't take your eyes off Mahoney's Flight for a moment. If the Fokker comes down, one of you should get him. If he doesn't show up, we'll keep it up until he does. It means long hours, but we can't help that. All clear? Good. Let's go and eat."

II

The following morning Mahoney was bringing his Flight back by way of Mossyface Wood as arranged. His altimeter registered 10,000 feet. Often he leaned back in his cockpit and studied the sky above him long and earnestly for a sign of Bigglesworth's Flight, but a film of cirrus-cloud far above concealed everything beyond it. Against that cloud a machine would show up like a beetle on a white ceiling; his roving eyes searched it, section by section, from horizon to horizon, but not a speck broke its pristine surface. At 6.30 he turned his nose for home according to plan, maintaining his height until he reached the line and only taking his eyes from aloft to see that Manley and Forest in the other two Camels were in place. He crossed the line in the inevitable flurry of archie, and started a long glide towards the aerodrome. A cluster of black archie bursting far away to the north showed where some allied machines were moving; there was apparently nothing else in the sky, yet he felt uneasy. What was the other side of that cloud? He wished he could see. Every fibre of his war-tried airman's instinct reacted against that opaque curtain. He flew with his eyes ever turned upwards. Suddenly he caught his breath. For a fraction of a second a black spot had appeared against the cloud and disappeared again almost before he could fasten his eyes on it. Keeping his eyes on the spot he raised his left arm, rocked his wings, opened up his engine, and warmed his guns with a short burst. What was going on up there?

He was soon to know. A machine, whether friend or foe he could not tell, wrapped in a sheet of flame, hurtled downwards through the cloud to oblivion, leaving a long plume of black smoke in its wake. Mahoney stiffened in his seat. Next came a Camel spinning wildly out of control. Then another Camel, streaking for home, followed by five Fokkers. Mahoney muttered through his clenched teeth and swung round and up in a wide arc, knowing as he did so that he could never get up to the Fokkers in time to help the Camel, now crossing the line at a speed which threatened to take its wings off. A barrage of archie appeared between the Fokkers and the Camel, and the black-crossed machines, after a moment's hesitation, turned and dived for home. Mahoney raced after the solitary Camel, whose pilot, seeing him coming, throttled back to wait for him.

They landed together and the C.O. ran out to meet them. Bigglesworth, the pilot of the lone Camel, was out first. "I've lost Swayne and Maddison," he said grimly, as the others joined him. "I've lost Swayne and Maddison," he repeated. "I've lost Swayne and Maddison; can't you hear me?" he said yet again. "What are you looking at me like that for?"

"Nobody's looking at you, Biggles," broke in the C.O. "Take it steady and tell us what happened."

Biggles groped for his cigarette-case. "We're boobs," he muttered bitterly. "Pilots, eh? We ought to be riding scooters in Kensington Gardens. What did we do? We did just what they knew we'd do; and they were waiting for us, the whole bunch of 'em!" He passed his hand over his face wearily as his passion spent itself. He tossed his flying-coat on to the tarmac and went on quietly: "I was up to 20,000 or as near as I could get, waiting. So were they, but I didn't see 'em at first; must have been hiding in that murk. I saw Mahoney coming, heading for Mossyface, and then I saw the White Fokker, by himself. He wasn't there for you, Mahoney; he was there to get me down. I didn't look up and that's a fact. I saw the Fokker going down and I went down after him. Where the others came from I don't know. They were into us just before we hit the cloud. The first thing I saw was the tracer, and poor Mad going down in flames next to me. I went after the white bird like a sack of bricks, but I lost him in the cloud. Swayne had gone, so I made for home, and I'm lucky to be here. That's all." He turned and strode off towards the mess. Major Mullen watched him go without a word.

"I'll have a word with you, Mahoney, and you, Mac," he said, and together they entered the Orderly Room. "We've got to do something about this," he began briskly. "We shall all be for Home Establishment if it goes on. Bigglesworth's going to bits fast, but if he can get that Fokker it'll restore his confidence. We've lost three machines in two days and we are going to lose more if we don't stop that white devil."

Bigglesworth entered.

"Hullo, Biggles; sit down," said the C.O. quietly.

Biggles nodded. "I've been trying to work it out, sir," he began, "and this is my idea. First of all, you'll notice that this Fokker doesn't go for the leaders. He always picks on one of the rear men in the formation; you saw how he got Norman. All right. Tomorrow we'll do the usual patrol of three. Mahoney or Mac can lead and I'll be in the formation. I'll pretend I'm scared of everything and sideslip away from every archie burst. Coming home, I'll hang back and the others will go on ahead without me. That should bring him down. If he comes I'll be ready and we'll see who can shoot straightest and quickest. If he gets me—well—he gets me, but if he doesn't I'll get him. He'll have height of me, I know, and that's where he

holds the cards. I've got an idea about that, too. Someone
will have to take every available machine and wait upstairs
to keep the others off if they try to butt in. Don't make
a move unless they start coming down; let them make the
first move; that should give you height of 'em. I'm having
an extra tank put in my machine so that I'll have some
spare juice when he'll reckon I've none left, in case I want
to turn back."

The C.O. nodded. "That sounds all right to me," he
said. "I've only one thing to say, and that is, I'll take the
party up topsides. You can rely on me to keep anybody
busy who starts to interfere with your show. Good enough!
We'll try it in the morning."

III

The pink hue of dawn had turned to turquoise when
Mahoney turned for home at the end of the dawn-patrol.
One machine of his Flight was lagging back, and for the
hundredth time he turned and waved for it to close up,
smiling as he did so. Biggles had played the novice to
perfection. Even now, a bracket of archie sent him career-
ing wide from the formation. Mahoney's roving eyes were
never still; slowly and methodically they searched every
section of the air around, above, and below. Far from them
a Rumpler was making for home followed by a long line
of white archie, but he made no attempt to pursue it. Far
to the north-east a formation of D.H. Nines was heading
out into the blue; high above them he could just make
out the escorting Bristols. He gazed upwards long and
anxiously. He could see nothing, but he knew that somewhere in the blue void at least one formation of fighters
was watching him that very moment. Biggles, too, was
watching; he had pushed his goggles up to see better. Now
and then he dived a little to gain speed so that the watchers

above might think he was trying to keep in position. They were going home now; if the White Fokker was about today he would soon have to show up. The formation started to lose height slowly; Biggles warmed his gun every few minutes, but still kept up the pretence of bad flying.

They were well over the line now. The two other Camels had dropped to 5,000 feet, but he hung back slightly above them. Once he threw a loop to show his apparent relief at being safely back over his own side of the line. Dash it, why didn't the fellow come? The two other Camels were nearly a mile ahead when Biggles suddenly focused his eyes on a spot far above and held it. Was it, or was it not? Yes! Far above and behind him a tiny light flashed for an instant, and he knew it for the sun striking the planes of a machine; whether friend or foe he could not tell. He kept his eyes glued to the spot. He could see the machine now, a tiny black speck rapidly growing larger.

Biggles smiled grimly. "Here comes the hawk. I'm the sparrow. Well, we'll see."

The machine was plainly visible now, a Fokker D.VII. There was no sign of archie, so he concluded that the Fokker had shut his engine off and had not yet been seen from the ground.

He opened his throttle wide and put his nose down slightly in order to get as much speed as possible without alarming the enemy above. The Fokker was coming down now with the speed of light; a cluster of archie far above it showed that the pilot had cast concealment to the winds. Biggles pushed his nose down and raced for home. Speed —speed—speed—that was all he wanted now to take him up behind the Fokker. How near dare he let him come? Could the Fokker hit him first burst? He had to chance it. At 200 feet a stream of tracer spurted from the Fokker's Spandaus. Biggles moved the rudder-bar, and, as the bullets streamed between his planes, pulled the stick back into his stomach. Half-rolling off the top of the loop and looking swiftly for his adversary, he caught his breath as the Fokker swept by a bare ten feet away. He had a vivid impression of the face of the man in the pilot's seat, looking at him. Biggles was on its tail in a flash. Through his sights he saw it still climbing. *Rat-tat-tat*—he grated his teeth as he hammered at the gun, which had jammed at the critical moment.

The Fokker had Immelmanned and was coming back at him now, but Biggles was ready, and pulled his nose up to take it head-on. Vaguely, out of the corner of his eye, he saw another Fokker whirling down in a cloud of smoke and other planes above. The White Fokker swerved and he followed it round.

They were circling now, each machine in a vertical bank not a hundred feet apart, the Fokker slowly gaining height. Biggles thought swiftly. "Ten more circles and he's above me and then it's goodbye." There was one chance left, a desperate one. He knew that the second he pulled out of the circle the Fokker would be on his tail and get a shot at him. Whatever he did the Fokker would still be on his tail at the finish. If he rolled, the Fokker would roll too, and still be in the same position. If he spun, the Fokker would spin—there was no shaking off a man who knew his job; but if he shot out of the circle he might get a lead of three hundred feet, and if he could loop fast enough he might get the Fokker from the top of his loop as it passed underneath in his wake. If he was too quick they would collide; no matter, they would go to Kingdom Come together. A feeling of fierce exultation swept over him.

"Come on, you devil!" he cried. "I'll take your lead," and shot out of the circle. He shoved his stick forward savagely as something smashed through the root of the nearest centre-section strut, and then he pulled it back in a swift zoom. A fleeting glance over his shoulder showed the Fokker three hundred feet behind. He pulled the stick right back into his stomach in a flick loop and his eyes

sought the sights as he pressed his triggers. Blue sky—
blue sky—the horizon—green fields—where was the Fokker? Ah! There he was, flying straight into his stream
of tracer. He saw the pilot slump forward in his seat. He
held the loop a moment longer and then flung the Camel
over on to even keel, looking swiftly for the Fokker as he
did so. It was rocketing like a hard-hit pheasant. It stalled;
its nose whipped over and with the engine racing it roared
down in an almost vertical dive. Biggles saw the top plane
fold back, and then he looked away feeling suddenly limp
and very tired.

A mile away five straight-winged machines were making
for the line, followed by four Camels; another Camel was
trying to land in a ploughed field below. Even as he
watched it the wheels touched and it somersaulted; a
figure scrambled out and looked upwards, waving. Biggles
sideslipped down into the next field and landed. Major
Mullen, the pilot of the wrecked Camel, ran to meet him.

"Good boy!" he cried. "You brought it off."

THE PACKET

"Two no-trumps." Biggles, newly appointed to Captain's rank since his affair with the White Fokker, made the bid as if he held all the court-cards in the pack.

"Two diamonds," offered Quinan, sitting on his left.

Mahoney, Biggles' partner, looked across the table apologetically. "No bid," he said, wearily.

"Don't you ever support your partner?" complained Biggles. "You've sat there all the afternoon croaking 'No bid' like a parrot. You ought to have a gramophone record made of it, and keep it with your scoring block."

"Who are you grousing at?" fired up Mahoney. "Any fool could sit and chirp no-trumps if they held the paper you do. If you could only play the cards you hold we'd get a rubber sometimes, instead of being a thousand points down."

"What sort of a game do you call this, anyway?" broke in Batson, the fourth player. "Why don't you show each other your cards and have done with it?"

Major Mullen entered the anteroom. "I want you, Biggles, when you've played the hand. Stand by, everybody; it's clearing," he continued, addressing others in the room and referring to the steady drizzle which had washed out flying so far that day.

Biggles looked at the hand which his partner had laid on the table with disgust. The knave to two diamonds was his best suit. "Clearing, eh?" he said, grimly. "So am I. Holy smoke, what a mitt!" He was two down on the bid. He rose. "Tot it up," he invited his opponents. "I'll settle when I come back."

"No you don't; you settle now," snapped Batson. "Miller went West owing me seventy francs—you cough it up, Biggles."

Biggles reluctantly counted out some notes. "Take it and I'll starve," he grumbled. "We'll finish this last rubber when I come back." He followed Major Mullen to the Squadron office, where he found an officer awaiting them, whose red tabs showed that he came from a higher command.

"Captain Bigglesworth—Colonel Raymond," began the C.O. "This is the officer I was telling you about, sir."

Biggles saluted and eyed the stranger curiously. The Colonel looked at him so long and earnestly that Biggles ran his mind swiftly over the events of the last few days, trying to recall some incident which might account for the senior officer's presence. "Sit down, Bigglesworth," said the Colonel at last. "Smoke, if you like." Biggles sat and lit a cigarette.

"You are wondering why I've sent for you," began the Colonel. "I'll tell you. Frankly, I'm going to ask you to undertake a tough proposition."

Biggles stiffened in his chair.

"First of all," went on the Colonel, "what I am going to tell you is secret. Not a word to anybody, and I mean that. Not one word. Now, this is the position. You know, of course, that we have—er—agents—operatives—call 'em what you like—over the line. They are usually taken over by aircraft; sometimes they drop by parachute and sometimes we land them, according to circumstances. Sometimes they come back; more often they do not. Sometimes the pilot who takes them over picks them up at a prearranged spot at a subsequent date. Sometimes—but never mind—that doesn't concern you.

"A fortnight ago such an agent went over. He did not come back. We know, never mind how, that he obtained what he went to fetch, which was, to be quite frank, a

packet of plans. An officer went to fetch him by arrangement, but the enemy had evidently watched our man and
wired the field. When the F.E. pilot—it was at night—
got to the field it was a death-trap. The officer was killed
landing. The operative bolted, but was taken. We have
since received information that he has been shot. Before
he was taken he managed to conceal the plans, and we
know where they are. We want those plans badly—
urgently; in three days they will be useless."

"I see," said Biggles slowly, "and you want me to go
and fetch them?"

"If you will."

"May I ask roughly where they are?" said Biggles.

"You may," replied the Colonel; "they are near Ariet."

"Ariet?" cried Biggles. "Why, 297 and 287 Squadrons
are both nearer than we are; why not send them?"

"For two reasons," replied Colonel Raymond: "297
Squadron is equipped with D.H.9's and a 'nine' could
not get down in the field. Obviously, if it were possible, we
should send an F.E. over at night, but, unfortunately, a
night landing is out of the question. Only a single-seater
could hope to get in, and then only by clever flying. A
single-seater might just get into the field, collect the plans,
and get off again before the enemy arrived. We photographed the place at once, naturally. Here are the prints—
take a look at them." He tossed a packet of photographs
casually to Biggles. "The place is about two miles from
where the disaster occurred, and the poor fellow must have
been taken somewhere near that spot."

One glance showed Biggles that the Colonel had not
underestimated the difficulty. "From what height was this
taken?" he asked, holding up a photograph on which was
marked a small white cross.

"Six thousand feet," replied the Colonel. "The white
mark is the position of the packet. When our man knew
the game was up he shoved the plans down a rabbit-hole

E

at the foot of a tree in the corner of that field. His last act was to release a pigeon, pin-pointing the position. The bird could not, of course, carry the plans."

"Stout effort," said Biggles approvingly. "So the plans are in the corner of the field I land in. From this photo I should say that the field is about 150 yards long by 60 yards wide. I might just get in, but the wind would have to be right."

"It is right, now," replied the Colonel, softly but pointedly.

"Now?"

"Now!"

"What about 287 Squadron?" asked Biggles curiously. "Don't think I'm inquisitive, sir, but they've got S.E.5's and they are nearer than we are."

"If you must know," returned the Colonel, "we have already been to them. They have lost two officers in the attempt and we can't ask them for another. Neither of them reached the field; archie got one, and we can only suppose that enemy aircraft got the other. You will pass both crashes on the way."

"Thanks," said Biggles grimly. "I can find my way without them. It's about twenty miles over, isn't it?"

"About that, yes."

"All right, sir," said Biggles, "I'll go, but I'd like to ask one thing." He turned to Major Mullen. "Do you mind if I ask for MacLaren or Mahoney to watch me from upstairs? If they could meet me on the way home it might help. I shall be low coming home—cold meat for any stray Hun that happens to be about?" He turned to Colonel Raymond. "What would happen if I had to land with those plans on me?" he asked.

"I expect the enemy would shoot you," returned the Colonel. "In fact, I am sure they would."

"All right, sir," said Biggles, "as long as we understand. If my engine cuts out while I am over the other side those

plans are going overboard before I hit the deck. I don't
mind dying, but when I die I'll die sitting down, like an
officer and a gentleman—not standing with my back to
a brick wall. If I come back, I shall have the plans with
me—if they are still there."

"That's fair enough," agreed Colonel Raymond.

"May I take Mac and Mahoney with me to look after
the ceiling?" he asked the C.O.

"Any objection, sir?" asked Major Mullen.

"None, as far as I am concerned," replied the Colonel.

"Good; then I'll be off," said Biggles, rising. "Going to
wait for the plans, sir? I shall be back within the hour,
or not at all."

"I'll wait," said the Colonel gravely.

Major Mullen accompanied Biggles to the door. "Get
those plans, Biggles," he said, "and the Squadron's name is
on the top line. Fail—and it's mud. Goodbye and good
luck." A swift handshake and Biggles was on his way to
the sheds.

As he gave instructions for his Camel to be started up,
he noticed that the sun was already sinking in the west;
he could not expect more than an hour and a half of daylight. He turned towards the Mess, a burst of song greeting
him as he opened the door.

"Mac! Mahoney! Here a minute," he called.

"What's the matter now, you hot-air merchant?" growled
Mahoney as they advanced to meet him. "Can't you——?"
Biggles cut him short.

"Show on," he said crisply. "I'm going to Ariet—to
fetch a packet."

"To Ariet?" said Mahoney incredulously.

"You'll get a packet all right," sneered MacLaren, "but
why go to Ariet for it?"

"Never mind, I can't tell you," said Biggles. "Serious,
chaps, I'm going to land at Ariet. I shall go over high up,
but I shall be low coming home, right on the carpet most

of the way, in all probability. Shan't have time to get any height. I'm going straight there and, I hope, straight back. You can help if you will by watching things up topsides. I've got to bring something back besides myself or I wouldn't ask you, and that's a fact. It's a long way over —twenty miles—and I expect every Hun in the sky will be looking for me as I come back. If they spot you they may not see me. That's all," he concluded.

"What the——?" began Mahoney.

Biggles cut him short. "I'm off now," he announced. "May I expect to see you shortly?"

"Of course," said Mahoney. "I don't understand what it's all about and it seems a fool business to me." He glanced up and saw Colonel Raymond and Major Mullen walking towards the Mess. "Confound these brass-hats," he growled. "Why can't they stay at home on a dud day? Righto, laddie; see you presently."

Twenty minutes later, well over the line at 12,000 feet, Biggles scanned the sky anxiously. Far away to the right, 3,000 feet above him, a formation of "Fours" were heading towards the line after a raid; he hoped that they would prove an attractive lure for any prowling enemy aircraft.

Ariet lay just ahead and below; Biggles put his nose down and dived, his eyes searching for his objective. Two miles west of Ariet, the Colonel had said! Good heavens, there seemed to be hundreds of oblong fields two miles west of Ariet. He looked at the photograph, which he had pinned to his instrument-board, and compared it with the ground below. That must be the field, over there to the right. He spun to lose height more rapidly. Pulling out, he examined the field closely. An encampment seemed dangerously close—perhaps a mile away, not more. There was the field. He noticed two horses idling in a corner and looked anxiously at the row of poplars which stood like a row of soldiers at the far end. "If I do get into the field I shall be mighty lucky to get out of it again," he mused.

Fortunately the wind, as the Colonel had said, was blowing in the right direction, otherwise it would be impossible.

He was only a couple of hundred feet up now and he could see men running about the encampment; some were clustered in little crouching groups, and as he cut his engine off he heard the faint rattle of a machine-gun. He winced as something crashed through the fuselage behind him. "That's too close," he muttered, and in the same breath, "Well, here goes."

He did a swift S turn, then kicked out his left foot and brought the stick over in a steep sideslip. As he levelled out, the tops of the trees brushed his undercarriage wheels and he fishtailed desperately to lose height.

The poplars at the far end of the field appeared to race towards him and he held his breath as his wheels touched ground. A molehill now, and I somersault, he thought, savage with himself for coming in so fast. His tail dropped, the skid dragged, and he breathed again. Without waiting for the machine to finish its run he swung round towards the tree in the corner. That must be the one, he thought. Springing quickly from the cockpit he looked round—ah, there was the rabbit-hole! He was on his hands and knees in a second, arm thrust far down. Nothing!

For a moment he remained stupefied with dismay. Must be another hole—or another tree, he thought, frantically, as he sprang to his feet. Realizing that he was on the verge of panicking, he steadied himself with an effort, and ran towards the next tree; his foot caught in an obstruction and he sprawled headlong, but he was on his feet again in an instant, instinctively glancing behind him to ascertain the cause of his fall. It was a rabbit-hole—there was a cluster of them. Of course, there would be, he thought grimly, and thrust his hand into the nearest. Ah! His finger closed around a bulky object; he pulled it out; it was a thick packet of papers.

He raced towards the Camel. Two hundred yards away a file of soldiers with an officer at their head were coming at the double. He tossed the packet into the cockpit, swung himself into his seat, and the next instant was racing, tail up, down the field to get into the wind. His heart sank as he surveyed the poplars; they seemed to reach upwards to the sky. Can't be done, he told himself grimly. In one place there was a gap in the line where a tree had fallen; could he get between them? He thought not, but he would try.

Already the grey-clad troops were scrambling through the hedge below the poplars. He opened the throttle and shoved the stick forward. The tail lifted. Hop—hop—thank goodness, she was off! He held his nose down for a moment longer and then zoomed at the middle of the gap. He flinched instinctively as a sharp crackling stabbed his ears and the machine shivered; whether it was gunshots or breaking wings, he didn't know.

He was through, in the air, and he'd got the plans! He laughed with relief as he dodged and twisted to spoil the aim of the marksmen below. Dare he waste time trying to gain height? He thought not. He would never be able to get to a safe height. Better to stick at two or three thousand feet just out of range of small arms from the ground, race for home, and trust to luck. With every nerve vibrating he looked up, around and below; most of the time he flew with his head thrown back, searching the sky above and in front of him, the direction from which danger would come. Not a machine was in sight. Halfway home he had climbed to 4,000 feet; tail up, he raced for the line. Ten minutes! A lot could happen in the air in ten minutes. His eyes were never still; anxiously they roved the air for signs of enemy aircraft, or for Mahoney or MacLaren's Camels.

Where was the packet? He groped about the floor of the cockpit, but couldn't find it. It must have got under his seat and drifted down the fuselage out of reach. Instinctively he glanced at the rev. counter. If he had to force-land now the enemy would find the packet. Would they? He felt for his Very pistol and made sure that it was loaded. Provided I don't crash I can always set fire to her, he reflected; the plans will burn with the rest.

His eyes, still searching, suddenly stopped and focused on a spot ahead. His heart missed a beat and his lips curled in a mirthless smile. Across the sky, straight ahead, moving swiftly towards him, were a line of straight-winged aeroplanes. Fokkers! Six of them.

He looked above the Fokkers for the expected Camels, but they were not there. "All right," he muttered. "I'll take the lot of you; come on."

For perhaps a minute they flew thus, the Camel, cut off by the Fokkers, still heading for the line, with the distance rapidly closing between them.

"They'll get me. I can't fight that lot and get away with it," thought Biggles.

Even as the thought crossed his mind the enemy machines made a swift turn and started climbing for more height. A puzzled expression crossed Biggles's face as he watched the manœuvre. "What's the big idea?" he muttered. "They're making a lot of fuss about one poor solitary Camel. They behave as if they were scared of me."

Not since the first moment that he had spotted the enemy aircraft had Biggles taken his eyes off them; now, still following the Fokkers round, they stopped abruptly and he started with astonishment. Twenty feet away from his right wing-tip was a Camel. Mahoney, in the cockpit, pushed up his goggles and grinned derisively at him. Biggles looked to the left and saw another Camel; he recognized MacLaren's machine. He glanced behind him and saw two more Camels bringing up the rear.

Biggles almost felt himself turn pale. "Phew!" he breathed. "Where did they come from? And I never saw

them! Am I going blind? Suppose they had been Fokkers;
it would have been just the same, except that I'd be smoking
on the floor by now. No wonder the Fokkers swerved when
they saw this lot coming. Five against six," he mused,
"that's better. They'll come in now, but they'll have to be
quick to stop us; it isn't four miles to home." Already he
could see the British balloon line. "Good old Mac, good
old Mahoney!" he thought exultantly.

The Fokkers were coming in now, the leader dropping
on one of the rear Camels, which swung round like a whirl-
wind and nosed up to face its attack head-on. The other
Fokkers closely followed the first, and Mac and Mahoney
turned outwards to meet them. Biggles's hand gripped the
stick in a spasm of impotent rage at the realization that
he would have to run for it and leave them to do his fighting for him. Twice he half-turned and checked himself.
"I'll never take on another job like this as long as I live,"
he vowed.

Two Fokker triplanes passed him to the eastward, making
for the dog-fight now ranging behind him. He was low, and
against the sun they had not seen him. Thrusting aside
the temptation to take advantage of his ideal position for
attack, Biggles raced across the line, muttering savagely
to himself. He dare not trust himself to look back. Suppose they got Mac or Mahoney—he daren't think of it.
Drat that brass-hat and his messenger-boy errands, anyway.
Well, he was over the line now—safe—safe with his con-
founded packet. As the aerodrome loomed up he shifted
slightly in his seat for a better view. He moved his hand
to shift a lump which seemed to have formed in the cushion
on his seat and the lump came away in his hand. It was the
packet. "It must have fallen on the seat and I've been
sitting on it all the time—too worried to notice it," he
laughed. Then he put his nose down and dived for the
aerodrome; 100, 120, 150 ticked up on the speed-indicator.

Major Mullen and Colonel Raymond were standing on

the tarmac waiting for him; he could see the Colonel's red tabs. He took the joystick in his left hand and the packet in his right—100 feet—50 feet—30—he saw the Colonel duck as he flung the plans at him, and then, after a wild zoom, swung round in a climbing turn for the line.

As he neared the support trenches he saw three Camels coming towards him. He looked anxiously for Mahoney's blue propeller boss; it was not among them.

"They've got old Mahoney!" He swallowed a lump in his throat.

The three Camels turned and fell in line with him. Mac, in the nearest, flew closer and waved his hand and jabbed downwards. Looking down, Biggles saw a Camel with a smashed undercarriage standing crookedly among the shell-holes. By its side was a figure waving cap and goggles. Mahoney! He must have been shot up and just made the line, thought Biggles, as, with joy in his heart, he turned for home.

The C.O. was waiting for him on the tarmac when he landed.

"Don't you know better than to throw things at staff-officers?" he said, smiling. "The Colonel has dashed back to headquarters with your billet-doux; he has asked me to thank you and say that he will not forget today's work."

"You can tell him when you see him that I won't, either," grinned Biggles. "Come on, chaps, let's go and fetch Mahoney, and finish that rubber."

J-9982

BIGGLES hummed contentedly to himself as he circled slowly at 16,000 feet. He looked at his watch and observed that he had been out nearly two hours on a solitary patrol which had so far proved uneventful. I'll do another five minutes and then pack up, he decided.

Below him lay a great bank of broken alto-cumulus cloud. Detached solid-looking masses of gleaming white mist floated languidly above the main cloudbank. Not another plane was in the air, at least, not above the cloud, as far as he could see. Every few minutes he turned, and holding his hand before his eyes studied the glare in the direction of the sun long and carefully between extended fingers. If danger lurked anywhere it was from there that it would probably come. He examined the cloud-bank below in detail, section by section. His eyes fell on a Camel coming towards him, far below, threading its way between the broken masses of cloud, through which the ground occasionally showed in a blur of bluey-grey.

Biggles placed himself between the sun and the other Camel so that it would pass about a thousand feet below him. "You poor hoot," he thought, as he watched the machine disinterestedly. "If I was a Fokker you'd be a dead man by now. Ah, here comes his partner!"

A second Camel had emerged from the cloud-bank and was now rapidly overtaking the first. The pilot of the leading Camel was evidently wide-awake, for he turned back towards the second machine to allow it to overtake him. Biggles noted that the second Camel was slightly above the leading one and that instead of putting its nose down to line up with it, the pilot was deliberately climbing for more height.

The second Camel was not more than fifty feet behind the first when its nose suddenly dropped as if the pilot intended to ram it. "Silly ass," thought Biggles. "What fool's game is he playing? That's how accidents happen." He caught his breath in amazed horror as a stream of tracers suddenly spurted from the guns of the topmost Camel point-blank into the cockpit of the one below. The stricken machine lurched drunkenly; a tongue of flame ran down the fuselage; its nose dropped and it dived through the cloud-bank out of sight, leaving only a little dark patch of smoke to mark its going.

For a moment Biggles stared unbelievingly, his brain refusing to believe what his eyes had seen.

"What the . . . ?" he gasped, and then, thrusting his stick forward, dived on the murderer out of the sun. But the other Camel was diving too, the pilot evidently intending to get below the cloud to watch the result of his handiwork. Biggles noted that the pilot did not once look up, and he was barely thirty feet behind it and slightly to one side when it disappeared into the swirling mist. Biggles pulled up to avoid a collision.

"J-9982," he muttered aloud, naming the maker's number which he had seen painted in white letters on the fin of the diving machine. "J-9982," he repeated again. "All right, you swine, I'll remember you."

He circled for a moment and dived through a hole in the clouds, not daring to risk a collision in the opaque mist. He looked about him quickly as he pulled out below the cloud, but the Camel had disappeared. Far below he could see a long trail of black smoke where the fallen machine was still burning. For ten minutes he searched in vain, and then, feeling sick with rage and horror, he headed for the line. He wondered who was in the Camel which had been so foully attacked; he knew that it must be either from his own or 231 squadron, as they were the only Camel squadrons in that area. He landed, and taxied quickly towards the sheds, where a group of pilots lounged.

"Anybody about, Mac?" he almost snapped at Mac-Laren, who had walked over to meet him.

"Yes, Mahoney's out with Forest and Hall on an O.P.,"[1] replied MacLaren, looking at him curiously.

"Here they come now," he added, pointing to the sky in the direction of the line; "two of 'em, anyway."

Biggles watched the two machines land, and Mahoney and Forest climbed out of their cockpits. "Where's Hall, Mahoney?" he asked in a strained voice.

"About somewhere—won't be long, I expect—he went fooling off on his own after I'd washed out," answered the Flight-Commander.

"Towards Berniet?"

"Yes—why?"

"You can pack his kit—he won't be coming back," said Biggles slowly, with a catch in his voice. He turned on his heel and walked towards the Squadron office.

Major Mullen smiled as he entered. "Sit down, Biggles," he said, the smile giving way to a look of anxiety as he noted the expression on the pilot's face. "What's wrong, laddie?" he asked, moving quickly towards him.

Biggles told what he'd seen, while the C.O. listened incredulously. "Good heavens, Biggles," he said at the end, "what a hellish thing to do! What shall we do about it?"

"I'm going over to 231 Squadron to see if they know anything about that other machine," said Biggles shortly. "It was never one of ours."

"If it's a Hun we shall have to warn every Squadron along the line," exclaimed Major Mullen gravely.

"And the Hun will know he's spotted within twenty-four hours," sneered Biggles. "You know what their intelligence

[1] O.P.—Ordinary Patrol.

service is like. At the first word he'll change the number on the machine and then we shall be in a mess. We've got him taped as it is, and he doesn't know it. No! You leave this to me, sir; we've got to take a chance. We'll get him, don't you worry."

Twenty minutes later Biggles strode into the ante-room of 231 Squadron. A chorus of salutations, couched according to individual taste, greeted him.

"No, thanks—can't stay now," he replied curtly to a dozen invitations to have a drink.

"On the water-waggon, Biggles?" asked Major Sharp, the C.O.

"No, sir, but I've got several things to do and I don't want to waste time. I have a word for your private ear, sir."

"Certainly; what is it?" replied the Major at once.

"Have you got a Camel on your strength numbered J-9982?" inquired Biggles.

"I don't know, but Tommy will tell us. Tommy," he called to the Equipment Officer, "come here a minute. Do you happen to know if we have a machine numbered J-9982 on the station?"

"Not now, sir; but we had. That was Jackson's machine; he went west at the beginning of the month, you remember."

"Anybody see him crash?" asked Biggles.

"Don't think so, but I'll check up on the combat reports if you like. Speaking from memory, he went on a balloon-strafing show and never came back; yes, that was it."

"So that was it, was it," said Biggles slowly. "Righto, Tommy; many thanks."

Biggles took Major Sharp on one side and spoke to him earnestly for some minutes, the Major nodding his head as if in agreement.

"Right, sir," said Biggles at length. "We'll leave it like that. Goodbye, sir. Cheerio, Tommy—cheerio, chaps."

Major Mullen looked up as Biggles re-entered his office. "It was as I thought, sir," began Biggles. "A Hun is flying that kite."

"I can't believe a German pilot would do such a dastardly thing," said the Major, shaking his head.

"No ordinary officer would, of course," agreed Biggles. "I'll bet you anything you like he is in no regular squadron. None of the Richthofen Staffel would stand for that stuff any more than we would. But you'll find skunks in every mob if you look for 'em. The higher command wouldn't stand in a chap's way if he was low enough to do it. Maybe they've detailed somebody for the job for a special reason; you can never tell. One thing is certain. The pilots over the other side know all about it or they'd shoot him down themselves. He's got a private mark somewhere. The archie batteries must know it, too. He drops them a light or throws some stunt occasionally so that they'll know it's him and not open fire."

"I shall have to report it to Wing," said the Major seriously.

"Give me forty-eight hours, sir," begged Biggles, "and then you can do what you like. Report it to Wing and it will be known from Paris to Berlin and from Calais to Switzerland before the day's out. There won't be one Hun flying a Camel. Every Camel our archie batteries see will have a Hun in it, and they'll shoot at it. We'll be a blight in the sky—a target for every other pilot in the air to shoot at. A pretty mess that would be. Perhaps that is what the Huns are hoping for. Stand on what I tell you, sir; forget it for twenty-four hours, anyway, and you won't regret it. I'm going to talk to Mac and Mahoney, then I'm going over to look for this flying rat. I know his hunting-ground. I just want to see him once more—just once—through my sights." Biggles, breathing heavily, departed to look for the other Flight-Commanders.

He found them in the sheds and called them aside.

"Listen, chaps," he began, "there's a Hun flying a Camel over the line. His number is J-9-9-8-2, remember it. If you let your imagination play on that for a moment you'll realize just what it means. We've got to get him, and get him quick. It was he who got Hall—I saw him, the dirty cannibal."

MacLaren turned pale as death. Mahoney, his Celtic temper getting the better of him, spat a burst of profanity. His rage brought tears to his eyes.

"Well," said Biggles, "that's that, and it's enough; I'm going to look for him. You coming?"

"We're coming," said the two pilots together, grimly.

"All right. Now look, we've got to be careful. You can't shoot at a Camel like you would at a Hun. I'm going to paint my prop boss, centre-section and fin, blue. Sharp is painting all 231 Squadron machines like that, so we'll know 'em. He knows the reason, but none of his officers do. None of our fellows are leaving the ground until we come back. If you see a Camel *without* these markings it may be him. If he is over Hunland and not being archied, it's almost certain to be him; but look for the number on the fin before you shoot—J-9982. If you see a Camel wearing that number, shoot quick and ask questions afterwards. He was working over the Berniet sector when I saw him, and that is where I am going to look for him. I'm off now."

II

The sun was low in the western sky. Biggles, patrolling at 14,000 feet, yawned. He was tired. This was his fourth patrol. He seemed to have been in the sky all day—looking for a Camel without a blue prop-boss. He had seen Mac-Laren and Mahoney several times; they too were still searching. Biggles had found a Hanoverana and shot it down in flames at the first burst without satisfying the stone-cold desire to kill which consumed him. He had been attacked by three Tripehounds[1] and had returned the attack with such savage fury and good effect that they acknowledged their mistake by diving for home.

This should have improved his temper, but it did not. He wanted a certain Camel, and nothing would satisfy him until he had seen it plunging earthwards in flames, like its victim. He almost hoped neither Mac nor Mahoney would find it and rob him of the pleasure. He yawned again. He could hardly keep awake, he was so tired. "This won't do," he muttered, and leaned out of the cockpit to let the icy slipstream fan his cheeks. Three black dots appeared in front of him, and he had warmed his guns before he realised they were only oil spots on his goggles. He wiped them clean and for the hundredth time began a systematic scrutiny of the atmosphere in every direction.

It would be dark in half an hour. Already the earth was a vast well of blue and purple shadows. "It's a washout," he thought bitterly. "I might as well be getting home. He's gone to roost."

As without losing height he commenced a wide circle towards his own lines his eye fell on a tiny speck far over and heading still farther in over the British lines. Small as it was, he recognised it for a Camel.

"Mac or Mahoney going home, I expect," he said to himself. "Well, I'll just make one more cast."

The outer edge of his circle took him well over the enemy lines, and ignoring the usual salvo of archie he looked long and searchingly into the enemy's country. A cluster of black spots attracted his attention. He recognised it for the German archie and flew closer to ascertain the reason for it. Turning, he climbed steadily and kept his eye on the bursts. He could see two machines approaching, now, and the straight top wings and dihedral-angled lower planes told him they were Camels. A minute later

[1] *Fokker Triplanes.*

he could see that both had blue prop-bosses. Mac and Mahoney!

Suddenly he stiffened in his seat. Who was it then that he had seen far over his own lines? He was round in a flash, heading for the direction taken by the lone machine. Five minutes later he saw a machine coming towards him. It was a Camel! With his heart thumping uncomfortably with excitement he circled cautiously to meet it. His nostrils quivered when he was close enough to see that the prop-boss was unpainted and the leading edge of the centre-section was brown. An icy hand seemed to clutch his heart. Suppose he made a mistake! Suppose it was one of his own boys—out without orders? He daren't think about it.

The Camel was close now, the pilot waving a greeting, but Biggles's eyes were fixed on the fin. J- . . . . the num-bers seemed to run into each other. Was he going blind? He pushed up his goggles and looked again. J-9982, he read, and grated his teeth.

The Camel closed up until it was flying beside him; the pilot smiling. Biggles showed his teeth in what he imag-ined to be an answering smile. "You swine," he breathed: "you dirty, unutterable, murdering swine! I'm going to kill you if it's the last thing I do on earth." Something made him glance upwards. Five Fokker triplanes were coming down on him like bolts from the blue. "So that's it, is it?" he muttered. "You're the bait and I'm the fish. That's your game. Well, they'll get me, but you're getting yours first." Swiftly he moved the stick slightly back, sideways, and then forwards. "Hold that, you rat," he shouted as he pressed his triggers. *Rat-tat-tat-tat-tat-tat-tat-tat*. A double stream of glittering tracer poured into the false Camel's cockpit. The pilot slumped forward in his seat and the machine nosed downwards.

Beside himself with rage, Biggles followed it, the Fokkers forgotten. "Hold that—AND THAT"—he gritted through his teeth as he poured burst after burst at point-blank range. "Burn, you hound!" He laughed aloud as a streamer of yellow fire curled aft along the side of the fuselage.

The rattle of guns near at hand made him look over his shoulder. A Fokker was on his tail, Spandaus stuttering. Another Fokker roared past with a Camel apparently glued to its tail; and still another Fokker and Camel were circling in tight spirals above.

"Go to it, boys," grinned Biggles as he pulled the joystick right back into his stomach, and half-rolling off the top of the loop looked swiftly for the Fokker that had singled him out for destruction. *Rat-tat-tat-tat-*. . . . "Oh! there you are!" he muttered, as the Fokker, which had followed his manoeuvre, came at him again.

Biggles, fighting mad, flew straight at it, guns streaming lead. The German lost his nerve first and swerved, Biggles swinging round on its tail, guns still going. Without warning, the black-crossed machine seemed to go to pieces in the air, and Biggles turned to look for the others. He saw a Camel spinning—a Tripehound following it down. He thrust his joystick forward and poured in a long burst at the Fokker, which, turning like lightning and nearly standing on its tail, spat a stream of death at him. It stalled as Biggles zoomed over it.

Where were the others? Biggles looked around for the Camel he had seen spinning and breathed a sigh of relief when he saw it far below streaking for the line. A Fokker was smoking on the ground near the false Camel. Then he discovered another Camel flying close behind him. For the first time since the combat began he realised that it was nearly dark. Feeling suddenly limp from reaction he waved to his companion, and together they dived for the line, emptying their guns into the enemy trenches as they passed over. The Camel below had already crossed the line to safety.

Major Mullen was waiting anxiously for them when they landed.

"Have you been balloon-strafing, Biggles?" he asked, looking aghast at bullet-shattered struts and torn fabric.

"No, sir," replied Biggles, with mock dignity, "but I have to report that I have today shot down a British air-craft numbered J-9982, recently on the strength of 231 Squadron, and more recently the equipment of an enemy pilot, name unknown."

He broke into a peal of nerve-jangling laughter, which ended in something like a sob. "Get me a drink some-body, please," he pleaded. "Lord! I'm tired."

THE BALLOONATICS

Captain James Bigglesworth brought the Headquarters car to a halt within a foot of the Service tender which had just stopped outside the Restaurant Chez Albert in the remote village of Clarmes. As he stepped out of the car, Captain Wilkinson of 287 Squadron leapt lightly from the tender. Biggles eyed him with astonishment.

"Hullo, Wilks!" he cried. "What the deuce brings you here?"

"What are you doing here?" parried Wilkinson.

"I've come——" Biggles paused—"I've come to do some shopping," he said brightly.

"What a funny thing; so have I," grinned Wilkinson. "And as I was here first I'm going to be served first. You've missed the boat, Biggles."

"I'm dashed if I have," cried Biggles hotly. "Our crowd discovered it—you pull your stick back, Wilks, and let the dog see the rabbit."

"Not on your life," retorted Wilkinson briskly. "First come, first served. You go and aviate your perishing Camel." So saying he made a swift dash for the door of the estaminet; but he was not quite fast enough. Biggles tackled him low, brought him down with a crash, and together they rolled across the sun-baked earth.

Just how the matter would have ended it is impossible to say, but at that moment a touring car pulled up beside them with a grinding of brakes and Colonel Raymond of Wing Headquarters, eyed the two belligerent officers through a monocle with well-feigned astonishment.

"Gentlemen! Officers! No, I must be mistaken," he said softly, but with a deadly sarcasm that brought a blush to the cheeks of both officers. "Are there no enemy aircraft left in the air that you must bicker among yourselves on the high road. Come, come. Can I be of any assistance?" He left his car, bade his chauffeur drive on, and came towards them. "Now," he said sternly, "what is all this about?"

"That is the point, sir," began Biggles. "Yesterday morning Batty—that is, Batson, of my Flight—was coming back this way by road from a forced landing, and dropped in here for—er—well, I suppose, for a drink. During a conversation with the proprietor he learned that M. Albert had, some years ago, laid in a stock of lemonade at the request of the staff of an Englishman who had taken the Chateau d'Abnay for the season. When this man returned to England, Albert had some of the stuff left on his hands, and, as the local bandits do not apparently drink lemonade, it is still here. To make a long story short, sir, Batty—that is, Batson—found no fewer than fourteen bottles reposing under the cobwebs in the cellar—and going for the pre-war price of five francs fifty the bottle. Unfortunately Batty—I mean Batson—had only enough money on him to bring one bottle back to the Mess, so I slipped along this morning to get the rest. But it appears that Batty—that is, Batson—went to a guest night at 287 Squadron last night and babbled the good news—at least that is presumably what happened since I find Captain Wilkinson here this morning. I think you will agree, sir, that having been found by an officer of 266 Squadron the stuff should rightly belong to them," concluded Biggles, eyeing the would-be sharer of the spoils in cold anger.

"Well, well," said the Colonel after a brief pause, "if that is the cause of the trouble I can settle the matter for you. The lemonade has gone."

"Gone!" cried Biggles aghast. "All of it?"

"Yes, I fear so," replied the Colonel sadly.

"Can you understand the mentality of a man who would take the lot and leave none for anyone else," exclaimed Biggles bitterly. "Do you know who it was, sir?"

The Colonel paused for a moment before replying. "Well, as a matter of fact, it was me," he admitted, the corners of his mouth twitching.

Biggles turned red and then white. Wilkinson started a guffaw, which he turned into a cough as the Colonel's eye fell on him.

"You see," went on the Colonel, "I, too, was a guest at 287 Squadron Mess last night, and fearing that the bottles might fall into unappreciative hands I collected it on my way home. I have just come to pay for it."

Biggles breathed heavily, but said nothing. Colonel Raymond eyed him sympathetically, and then brightened as an idea struck him.

"Now, I'll be fair about this; I'll tell you what I'll do," he began.

"I know! Toss for it, sir," suggested Biggles eagerly, feeling in his pocket for a coin.

The Colonel shook his head. "No," he said. "I've a better idea than that; do you fellows know the Duneville balloon?"

Biggles showed his teeth in a mirthless smile. "Do I? I should say I do! When I'm tired of life I am going to fly within half a mile of that sausage. That's all that will be necessary."

Wilkinson nodded. "You won't have to go so far as that, Biggles," he said. "Go within a mile of that kite and you'll see Old Man Death waiting with the door wide open."

"In that case it doesn't matter," said the Colonel, preparing to enter the estaminet.

"Just a moment, sir! What about the balloon?" cried Biggles anxiously.

"Well, what I was going to suggest was this," replied the

Colonel. "Strictly between ourselves, the infantry are doing a show in the morning. We are moving a lot of troops, and that observation balloon has got to come down and stay down. I'm willing to hand over six bottles of lemonade, free, gratis and for nothing, to the officer who does most to keep that balloon on the floor for the next few hours. Today is Sunday. Time expires twelve noon tomorrow. We'll score like this. Forcing the ground-crew to haul the balloon down counts three points; shooting it down in flames, five points. My observers will have their glasses on the balloon all day. You know as well as I do that if you shoot the balloon down there will be another one up within a few hours. Duneville is an important observation post for the Boche."

"Did you say just now that you would be *fair*, sir?" asked Biggles incredulously.

Colonel Raymond ignored the thrust. "Pulled down—a try—three points; down in flames—goal—five points; don't forget." In the doorway of the estaminet he turned and a broad smile spread over his face. "Any officer taking the balloon prisoner scores a grand slam and gets the other six bottles. Goodbye."

For a full minute the two Flight-Commanders stood staring at the closed door as if fascinated; then Biggles started towards his car. With his foot on the running-board he turned to Wilkinson.

"You keep your glasshouse out of my way," he said curtly, referring to the S.E.5, which was, at that time, fitted with a semi-cabin windscreen.

"And you keep your oil-swilling 'hump' where it belongs," snapped Wilkinson, referring to Biggles's Camel.

Inside the estaminet Colonel Raymond was sipping a drink. Albert was packing twelve bottles into a case. "Unless I am very much mistaken," mused the Colonel, "that Boche balloon is in for a trying time—a very trying time."

II

An hour later, Biggles, clad in a leather coat, made his way to the hangars. In his pocket he carried written orders to strafe the Duneville Balloon; these orders permitted him to carry Buckingham (incendiary) bullets, forbidden on pain of death for any other purpose by the rules of war. Rules were seldom observed during the great struggle, but the order would, at least, protect him from trouble at the hands of the enemy, should he be forced to land on the wrong side of the lines. He halted before a Camel upon which a squad of ack-emmas were working feverishly.

"What are you doing, Flight?" he asked the Flight-Sergeant in charge.

"Just a top overhaul, sir, while you were away," replied the Flight-Sergeant. "She'll be ready in an hour."

Biggles frowned but said nothing. He was disappointed to find his machine wasn't ready, but he would not say anything to discourage the mechanics. "Fill the belts with tracer and Buckingham right through in that order," he said, presently, as he seated himself and prepared to wait.

"Going balloon-strafing, sir?"

Biggles nodded.

The Sergeant shrugged his shoulders and said no more.

The machine was ready at last. Biggles, fretting with impatience, took off and headed for the line, climbing all the time in the direction of Duneville. It did not take him many minutes to spot his objective. There it was, the mis-shapen beast, four miles away and five thousand feet below him. Circling cautiously towards it he examined the air and ground in its vicinity carefully. He could see nothing, but he knew perfectly well that once let him venture within a mile of that sausage floating so placidly in the blue vault, the air about it would be a maelstrom of fire and hurtling metal. He started. Far above the balloon appeared a tiny black speck surrounded by a halo of black smoke and little darting jabs of flame. Biggles whistled and raced towards the scene, watching the machine, which he now recognised as an S.E.5, with interest. "Sweet spirits of nitre," he muttered. "What a hell to be flying through, all for a case of lemonade. He must be crazy."

The S.E.5 was going down in an almost vertical dive, twisting like a wounded sparrow-hawk, pieces of torn fabric streaming out behind it. Swift as had been its descent the balloon crew were faster, and the sausage was on the ground before the S.E. could reach it. The machine pulled up in an almost vertical zoom, and as it flew past him, Wilkinson, the pilot, pushed up his goggles and then very deliberately jabbed up three fingers at him.

"Three points, eh," muttered Biggles. He placed his thumb against his nose and extended his fingers in the time-honoured manner. Wilkinson grinned, and with a parting wave turned for home. Biggles climbed away disconsolately.

For an hour he circled round, returning at intervals to see if the balloon had reappeared, but there was no sign of it, and he knew the reason. "They can see me," he pondered. "They know why I'm hanging around, presently they'll send for a Staffel[1] of Huns to drive me away. I'll have to try different tactics."

He returned to the aerodrome, refuelled, and returning to the line crossed over four or five miles from the balloon-station. For ten minutes he flew straight into the enemy's country and then circled back to approach the balloon from its own side of the line. Looking ahead anxiously, his heart leapt as his eyes fell in the ungainly gas-bag floating below him. Instinctively he looked upwards to make sure that there were no protecting machines, and caught his breath sharply.

[1] The German fighting squadrons were known as Jagdstaffeln.

Three Fokker Triplanes were coming down in a steep dive, but not in his direction. Following their line of flight he saw an S.E.5, which, apparently, just realising its danger, was streaking for home.

"That's Wilks," thought Biggles, "Wilks for a certainty. He did the same thing as I've done and was just going for the sausage when he saw them coming. They'll get him. They've 3,000 feet of height of him—he'll never reach the line. The Tripehounds have left the coast clear for me, though; I'll never get such a chance again. It's Wilks or the balloon—dash the luck!—I can't let them get old Wilks."

He put his nose down in the wake of the Fokkers in a wire-screaming dive. He reached the nearest Fokker almost at the same time as the leading Fokker fired at the S.E.5. At that moment the black-crossed machines were too intent on their quarry to look back. Biggles held his fire until his propeller was only a few feet from the nearest enemy machine, and then raked it from tail-skid to propeller-boss with one deadly burst. The Triplane slowly turned over on to its back. Hearing the shots, the other two Fokkers whirled round, leaving the S.E. a clear run home. Biggles, cold as ice, was on the tail of the nearest in a flash, and the next instant all three machines were turning in a tight circle. The Fokkers started to outclimb him at once, as he knew they would. "I'm in a mess now," he thought, as the top Fokker levelled out to come down on him, and he pulled the Camel up to take it head-on.

What was that? An S.E.5 was above them all, coming down like a comet on the Fokker, guns streaming two pencil-lines of white smoke. The Fokker turned and dived, the S.E. on its tail.

"Good for you, Wilks," grinned Biggles; "that evens things up."

He looked for the other Triplane, but it was a mile away far over its own side of the line. Then he remembered the balloon. Where was it? Great Scott! There it was, still up, less than a mile away. Even as Biggles put his nose down towards it, its crew seemed to divine his intention and started to haul it down. A stabbing flame and a cloud of black smoke appeared in front of him, but he did not alter his course. He was flying through a hail of archie and machine-gun bullets now, every nerve taut, eyes on the blurred mass of the balloon. Five hundred feet—three hundred—one hundred—the distance closed between them.

"At least I won't be out for a duck," he muttered, as he pressed his triggers. He had a fleeting vision of the observers' parachutes opening as they sprang from the basket, a great burst of flame, and then he was twisting upwards in a wild zoom in the direction of the line.

He breathed a sigh of relief as he passed over. An S.E.5 appeared by his side, the pilot waved a greeting. Biggles pulled off his gauntlet and jabbed five fingers upwards. "There will be no more balloons today," he said to himself, glancing towards the setting sun, as he made for home.

As he landed, "Watt" Tyler, the Recording Officer, handed him a slip. "Signal for you from Wing H.Q., just in," he said. "Dashed if I know what it means."

Biggles glanced at the message and smiled.

"Score 5–3 your favour," he read. The initials were those of Colonel Raymond.

III

"Tired of life, Biggles?"

Biggles looked up from the combat report to see Major Mullen eyeing him sadly.

"Why, sir?" he asked.

"You've been balloon-strafing," said the C.O.

"That's true, sir. I had a little affair with the Duneville sausage this afternoon," admitted Biggles.

"I see," said the C.O. "Well, if you're in a hurry to write yourself off,[1] go right ahead. You get balloon fever and you won't last a week; you know that as well as I do. Don't be a fool, Biggles. Let 'em alone. By the way, I see that the wind has shifted; blowing straight over our way for a change. All right, finish your report, but let those infernal kites alone," he added as he left the room.

Biggles remained with his pen poised, as an idea flashed into his mind. The wind was blowing straight over our lines, was it? He hurried to the window and looked at the wind-stocking. "Lord, so it is!" he muttered, and sat down, deep in thought. What was it Colonel Raymond had said? "Anybody capturing the balloon scores a grand slam and gets the other six bottles." "Great Scott!" he grinned. "I wonder if it's possible? If I could cut the cable the balloon would drift over to our side. Cables have been cut by shell splinters before today. I wonder——!"

He dashed off to the nearest balloon squadron and after spending half an hour asking many questions in the company of a balloon officer, returned to the aerodrome still deep in thought. He sought his Flight-Sergeant.

"What bombs have we, Flight?" he asked.

"Only 20-lb. Coopers, sir," replied the N.C.O., looking at him queerly.

"Nothing bigger?"

"No, sir."

"I see. Do you think my Camel would carry a 112-pounder?"

"Carry it all right, sir, if you could get the rack fixed,

[1] *"Write-off." An aeroplane that was so badly damaged as to be of no further use was officially "written-off" the squadron books. The expression "write-off" was loosely used to infer the complete destruction of anything.*

though you wouldn't be able to throw the machine about much with that lot on," returned the Flight-Sergeant.

"Where can we get one?"

"297 Squadron at Arville use them on their 'Nines,'[1] sir. If you gave me a chit to the E.O.[2] I could fetch one and borrow a bomb-rack."

"Will you do that for me, Flight—and get it fixed to-night? I'm leaving the ground at daylight in the morning. I'd like a five-seconds 'delay' fuse fixed, if you can manage it."

"I'll have a shot at it, sir."

Well satisfied with his evening's work, Biggles went to bed early.

IV

At the first streak of dawn he was in the cockpit warming up his engine. The Flight-Sergeant, as good as his word, had hung the bomb under the fuselage just clear of the undercarriage. The change of wind had brought low cloud, and Biggles looked at it anxiously. Too much cloud would spoil visibility and the balloon would not go up.

The Camel took a long run to lift its unusual load, but once in the air the difference was hardly noticeable except for a slight heaviness on the controls. "This is the maddest thing I've ever done in my life," soliloquized the pilot, as he sped towards the lines.

As he approached Duneville he saw the balloon just going up, but following his tactics of the previous day he circled, crossed the line a few miles lower down, and prepared to attack from the German side. The balloon was straight ahead of him now and Biggles exclaimed softly as his eye fell on a solitary S.E.5 farther west, trailing a line of archie bursts in its wake. He put the nose

[1] D.H.9s.   [2] Equipment Officer.

of the Camel down and started "hedge-hopping" in the direction of the sausage, now far above him. Vaguely he heard the crackle of machine-gun fire as he raced across the enemy reserve trenches, but he heeded it not. He was afraid of one thing only, and that was accidentally hitting the balloon-cable with his wing; it was only about as thick as his finger and would be difficult to see. The balloon was less than a mile away now, the ground-party no doubt looking upwards for any possible danger. With his wheels nearly touching the ground he tore towards the little group at the foot of the cable. He saw them turn in his direction, scatter and dive for shelter, and then he was on them. At the last instant he threw the machine in a bank away from the cable-drum, pulled the bomb-toggle, and zoomed, twisting and turning as he dashed towards his own lines. As he reached comparative safety he looked back over his shoulder; a great pillar of smoke marked the spot where the bomb had burst, but the sausage was nowhere in sight.

Ignoring the archie that still followed him, Biggles pushed up his goggles and looked again, an expression of incredulous amazement on his face. A movement far above caught his eye and caused him to look up; an ejaculation of astonishment escaped his lips. The balloon, freed from its anchor, had shot up to ten or eleven thousand feet and was already sailing over no-man's land! He could see no parachutes, and concluded that the observers, taken unawares, were still in the basket. Far away he saw an S.E.5 diving across the line to where the balloon would normally be. Biggles grinned. "The bird has flown," he muttered, as the S.E. pilot swung round in obvious confusion, evidently at a loss to know what had become of it; but when he began climbing Biggles knew that his balloon had been sighted by the lynx-eyed Flight-Commander.

Biggles reached the balloon first, waved a greeting to the occupants, who were busy with something inside the basket, and then fired a warning Very light in the direction of the rapidly approaching S.E.5. He guessed what had happened to the balloon. When the mooring cable had been cut it had shot up until the automatic valve had functioned, and, by releasing the gas, checked the ascent, and incident-ally prevented the balloon from bursting. The observers had been too startled to take to their parachutes im-mediately, and then, seeing that they would in any case drift across the line and be taken prisoners, decided to remain where they were and bring their unwieldy craft to earth.

They were now opening the valve and losing height rapidly, which was exactly what Biggles had hoped would happen. He knew little of ballooning, but enough to understand what the two men in the basket would do. The balloon would drop with increasing rapidity. Near the ground the crew would check its descent by throwing ballast overboard and then pull the rip-panel, releasing all the gas from the envelope, which would then collapse and sink lightly to earth.

It happened as he anticipated. Close to the ground the fabric spread out like a giant mushroom and quietly settled down. Biggles landed in the next field, the S.E.5 landing a moment later. A touring car intercepted them as they crossed the road separating them from the deflated monster. Colonel Raymond greeted them.

"Who did that?" he laughed, pointing towards the balloon.

"My prisoner, sir," grinned Biggles. "I claim a grand slam and the twelve bottles. There will be no more balloons up at Duneville today."

"You've won them," laughed the Colonel. "Collect them at the Chez Albert. They are paid for."

"At the where?" said the two pilots together, staring. "Do you mean to tell us that the stuff was in there all the time?" added Biggles, with a marked lack of respect.

The Colonel nodded, his eyes twinkling. "Why were you so anxious to have it?"

Biggles answered: "You see, it's 266 guest-night to-morrow, and I thought we'd give everyone a treat. Will you come, sir? You will, Wilks, I know."

"You bet I will!" cried both officers together.

THE BLUE DEVIL

THE summer sun shone down from a sky of cloudless blue. Biggles sat on a doorstep of No. 287 Squadron Mess and watched the evolutions of an aeroplane high overhead with puzzled interest, wondering what the pilot was trying to do.

He was on his way home from an uneventful morning patrol and had dropped in to have a word or two with Wilkinson, only to be told that he was in the air.

Slightly torpid from two hours at 16,000 feet, he had settled down in the ante-room to await his return, when the amazing aerobatics of the S.E.5 above had attracted his attention. With several other officers he had moved to the door in order to obtain an uninterrupted view of the performance.

"That's Wilks all right," observed Barrett, a comparative veteran of six months at the front. "He's been doing that on and off for the last two days."

Biggles nodded wonderingly. "What's the matter with him?" he asked. "I always thought he was crazy—just look at the fool; he'll break that machine in a minute."

The evolutions of the S.E.5 were certainly sufficiently unusual to call for comment. The pilot appeared to be trying to do something between a vertical bank and a half-roll. Over and over he repeated the same manoeuvre, sometimes falling out of it into a spin and sometimes in a stall.

"Here he comes; you can ask him," said Barrett, as the engine was cut off and the S.E.5 commenced to glide down to land.

Biggles strolled across the tarmac to meet the pilot.

"How did that look from the ground?" asked Wilkinson, grinning, as he clambered out of the cockpit.

"It looked to me that if you were trying to strip the wings off that kite you must have jolly nearly succeeded," replied Biggles. "Are you tired of life or something? What's the big idea, anyway?"

"Come across to the mess and I'll tell you," answered Wilkinson, and together they made their way towards the ante-room.

"Now tell me this," continued the S.E.5 pilot when they had called for drinks and made themselves comfortable; "have you ever bumped into that blue-and-yellow Boche circus that hangs out somewhere near Lille? I believe they are now on Aerodrome 27."

"Too true I have," admitted Biggles. "What about them?"

"Have you seen 'em lately?"

"No! Come on; cough it up, laddie. Have they turned pink, or what?"

"No, they're still blue, but they've got a new leader, and if you place any value at all on your young life keep out of his way, that's all," replied Wilkinson soberly.

"Hot stuff, eh?" inquired Biggles.

"He's hotter than hell at twelve noon on midsummer's day," declared Wilkinson. "Now, let me tell you something else. First of all, as you know, these Albatroses are all painted blue, but there's a bit of yellow on them somewhere."

"Yes, I've noticed that," replied Biggles. "One of them has got yellow elevators, and there's another with a yellow centre-section."

"That's right," agreed Wilkinson. "They've all got that touch of yellow on them somewhere—that is, all except the leader. That's what I'm told by one or two fellows who have seen him and lived to tell the tale. He's blue

all over—no yellow anywhere. Blue propeller-boss, wheel-discs—everything, in fact. That marks him for you.
The Huns call him the Blue Devil and they say he's got thirty victories in two months—every machine he's ever tackled. That's pretty good going, and, if it's true, he must be pretty smart. The most amazing thing about it is, though, they say his machine has never been touched by a bullet."

"Who says?" inquired Biggles curiously.

"Wait a minute; don't be in such an infernal hurry. Now, until a couple of days ago we had only heard rumours about this bloke, but last Thursday I got one of his men, an N.C.O. pilot. I met him over Passchendaele and we had a rough-house. In the end I got his engine. For once the wind was blowing our way and we had drifted a bit in the scrap. To cut a long story short, he landed under control behind our lines. He managed to set fire to his machine before anybody could get to him, but we brought him back to the mess for a drink—you know. We made a wild night of it and under the influence of alcohol he started bragging, like a Boche will when he's had a few drinks. Among other things, he told us that this Blue Bird is going to knock down every one of our machines one after the other, just like that. Now listen to this. This Hun has got a new stunt which sounds like the Immelmann business all over again. You remember that when Immelmann first invented his turn, nobody could touch him until we rumbled it, and then McCubbin got him. Everybody does the stunt now, so it doesn't cut much ice. Nobody knows quite what this new Hun does or how he does it. He's tried to explain it to his own chaps, but they can't get the hang of it, which seems funny, I'll admit. This lad I got tried to tell me how it was done—that is, the stick and rudder movements; but I couldn't follow how it worked. I've tried to do it in the air; you saw me trying just now. It's a new sort of turn; just when you get on this fellow's tail and kid yourself you've got him cold, he pivots somehow on his wing-tip and gets *you*. This lad of mine swore that the man who gets on his tail is cold meat—dead before he knows what's hit him. It sounds mighty unlikely to me, but then the Immelmann turn probably sounded just as unlikely in its day. Well, that's the story, laddie, and now you know as much about it as I do. The point is, what are we going to do about it?"

Biggles pondered for a few moments. "The thing seems to be for us to find him and see how he does it," he observed in a flash of inspiration.

"I thought you'd get a rush of blood to the brain," sneered Wilkinson. "You get on his tail and I'll do the watching."

"Funny, aren't you?" retorted Biggles. "If I meet him I'll do my own watching and then come back and tell you all about it. Maybe you'll be able to earn your pay and get a Hun or two occasionally. Blue devils go pop at the end, if I remember my fireworks."

On his way home Biggles thought a good deal about what Wilkinson had told him concerning the blue Albatros. "Sooner or later I shall meet him," he reflected, "so I might as well decide how I am going to act. When he pulls his patent stunt he must reckon on the fellow he's fighting doing the usual thing, making a certain move at a certain time, and up to the present the fellow has always obliged him; but if he happened to do something else, something unorthodox, it might put him off his stroke. Well, we'll see; but it's difficult to know what to do if you don't know what the other fellow's going to do. If I could see the trick once I should know, but apparently he takes care that nobody gets a second chance."

His curiosity prompted him to spend a good deal of time in the Lille area, but his vigilance was unrewarded; of the blue circus he saw no sign. He saw Wilkinson several times, and each time he learned that the Blue Devil had claimed another victim, but the knowledge only sharpened his curiosity.

By the perversity of fate it so happened that the encounter occurred at a moment when no thought of it was in his mind. He was returning home from a lone patrol at 15,000 feet, deliberating in his mind as to whether or not he should have a shot at the new Duneville Balloon as he crossed the lines, when his ever-watchful eye saw a grey shadow flit across a cloud far below. It was only a fleeting glimpse, but it was sufficient. It was not his own shadow. What, then? More from instinct than actual thought he whirled and flung stick and rudder-bar hard over as the rattle of guns struck his ears. An Albatros screamed past him barely twenty feet away. Biggles was on its tail in a flash, and only then did he notice its colour.

It was blue! Biggles caught his breath as he ran his eyes swiftly over it, looking for a touch of yellow, but there was none. "So it's you, is it?" he muttered, as he tore after it, trying vainly to bring his sights to bear. "Well, let's see the trick."

He was as cold as ice, every nerve braced, for unless rumour lied he was up against a foeman of outstanding ability, a man who had downed thirty machines in as many duels without once having his own machine touched.

Biggles knew that he was about to fight the battle of his life, where one false move would mean the end. Neither of them had ever been beaten, but now one of them must taste defeat. In a few minutes either a Camel or an Albatros would be hurtling downwards on its way to oblivion. He tightened his grip on the joystick and warmed his guns with a short burst.

Both machines were banking vertically now, one each side of a circle not a hundred feet across. Round and round they raced as if swinging on an invisible pivot, the circle slowly decreasing in size. Tighter and tighter became the spiral as each pilot tried to see the other through his sights.

The wind screamed in his wires and Biggles began to feel dizzy with the strain; he had lost all count of time and space, and of the perpendicular. His joystick was right back in his thigh as he strove to cut across a chord of the circle and place himself in a position for a shot. Always just in front of his nose was the blue tail, just out of reach; just far enough out of his field of fire to make shooting a waste of ammunition. Another few inches would do it. The ring of his sight cut across the blue tail now—oh, just for a little more—just another inch! "Come on, where's your trick?" snarled Biggles, feeling that he was getting giddy.

He was ready for it when it happened, although just how it came about he could never afterwards tell. At one moment his sights were within a foot of the blue cockpit; he saw the Boche turn his head slowly, and the next instant the blue nose was pointing at him, a double stream of scarlet flame pouring from the twin Spandau guns.

Biggles knew that he was caught—doomed. He heard bullets tearing through the fuselage behind him and the sound seemed to send him mad. Unconsciously he did the very thing he had planned to do—the unorthodox. Instead of trying to get out of that blasting stream of lead, thereby giving himself over to certain death, he savagely shoved the stick forward and tried to ram his opponent, pressing his triggers automatically as his nose came in line with the other's.

For perhaps one second the two machines faced each other thus, not fifty feet apart, their tracer making a glittering line between them. Biggles had a fleeting glimpse of the Albatros jerking desperately sideways; at the same instant something snatched at the side of his sidcot and a hammer-like blow smashed across his face; he slipped off on to his wing and spun. He came out of the spin tearing madly at the smashed goggles which were blinding him, spun again, and then righted the machine by sheer instinct.

Half-dazed, he wiped the blood from his eyes and looked around for the machine which he knew must be coming in for the coup-de-grâce. It was nowhere in sight. It was some seconds before he picked it out, half-way to the ground, spinning viciously.

Biggles leaned back in his cockpit for a moment, sick and faint from shock and reaction. When he looked down again the black-crossed machine was a flattened wreck on the ground. Gently he turned the torn and tattered Camel for home. "That was closish," he muttered to himself, "closish. I shall have to be more careful. I wonder how he did that stunt? Pity Wilks wasn't watching!"

CAMOUFLAGE

FROM his elevated position in the cockpit of a Camel, Biggles surveyed the scene below him dispassionately. An intricate tracery of thin white lines marked the trench system where half a million men were locked in a life-and-death struggle, and a line of tiny white puffs, looking ridiculously harmless from the distance, showed the extent of the artillery barrage of flame and steel.

He turned eastward into enemy country and subjected every inch of the sky to a searching scrutiny. For a few minutes he flew thus, keeping a watchful eye upwards and occasionally glancing downwards to check his landmarks. During one of these periodical inspections of the country below something caught his eye which caused him to prolong his examination; he tilted his wing to see more clearly.

"Well, I'm dashed," he muttered to himself; "funny I've never noticed that before."

The object that had excited his curiosity was commonplace enough; it was simply a small church on a slight eminence. His eye followed the winding road to where it crossed the main Lille road and thence to the small hamlet of Bonvillier, which the church was evidently intended to serve.

"I could have sworn the church was in the middle of the village," he thought. "So it is," he said aloud, as his eye fell on a square-towered building in the market-place. "Two churches, eh? They must have religious mania. I expect the other is a chapel; funny I've never noticed it before. It's plain enough to see, in all conscience."

He turned back towards the lines, and after another penetrating examination of the surrounding atmosphere glanced at his map to pin-point the chapel. It was not shown. He made a wide circle, wing down, sideslipping to lose height quickly, and ignoring the inevitable salvo of archie took a closer look at the building which had intrigued him. Pretty old place, he commented, as he picked out the details of the ivy-covered masonry, the crumbling tombstones and the neat flower-beds that bordered the curé's residence.

An exceptionally close burst of archie reminded him that he was dangerously low over the enemy lines, and as he was at the end of his patrol he dived for home, emptying his guns into the Boche support-trenches as he passed over them.

Arriving back at the aerodrome, he landed and made his way slowly to the Squadron Office. Colonel Raymond, of Wing Headquarters, who was in earnest conversation with Major Mullen, the C.O., broke off to nod a greeting.

"Morning, Bigglesworth," he called cheerfully.

"Good morning, sir," replied Biggles. "No more packets for me to fetch, I hope," he added with a grin.

"No," responded the Colonel seriously. "But I'm a bit worried, all the same. We can't locate that heavy gun the Boche are using against our rest-camps. I've had every likely area photographed, but we can't find the blaze[1] anywhere. Haven't seen a loose gun about, I suppose?"

Biggles shook his head. "I haven't seen a thing the whole morning," he replied bitterly, "except a church I didn't know existed." He took a pencil off the Major's desk and marked the position carefully on his map.

The Colonel, glancing over his shoulder, smiled with

[1] *Blaze. The line of burnt or flattened grass in front of the muzzle of a gun, caused by the flash. It showed up plainly in air photographs and betrayed many batteries.*

superior wisdom. "You've got that wrong," he said; "there's no church there."

Mahoney and several other officers entered the room to write their combat reports, but Biggles heeded them not.

"What do you mean, sir?" he asked, a trifle nettled. "I know a church when I see one."

"What sort of a church is it?" asked Colonel Raymond. Biggles described it briefly.

"Why, that's the church on the hill at Berniet," smiled the Colonel.

"Berniet!" cried Biggles. "But I haven't been near Berniet this morning. I beg your pardon, sir, but I saw that church here," and he indicated the position at Bonvillier, emphatically, with the point of a pencil.

Colonel Raymond shook his head. "Look," he said suddenly, and, selecting a photograph from a folio on the table, passed it across. "These photos were taken yesterday. There is Bonvillier, there are the crossroads—there's no church, as you can see."

Biggles stared at the photographs in comical amazement, and then frowned.

"You're wrong, Biggles; there's no church there," broke in Mahoney.

Biggles wheeled round in a flash. "Are you telling me that I can't read a map, or that I don't know where I am when I'm flying?" he snapped.

"Looks like it," grinned the other Flight-Commander, frankly, amid laughter.

Biggles sprang to his feet, white with anger. "Funny, aren't you?" he sneered. "All right; we'll see who's right."

He went out and slammed the door behind him.

II

On a dawn patrol the following morning he flew straight to Bonvillier and looked down confidently for the church. His eye picked out the white ribbon of road. "There's the cross-roads—the village—well, I'm dashed!" He stared as if fascinated at the spot where, the day before, he thought he had located the sacred building. He pushed up his goggles and examined both sides of the road minutely, but only empty fields met his gaze. "I'm going crazy," he told himself bitterly. "I'll soon be for H.E.[1] at this rate; I'm beginning to see things. Well, it isn't there. Let's have a look at Berniet."

Ten minutes later he was circling high above the other village looking for the church, but in vain. Suddenly he laughed. "Pretty good; we're all wrong; it isn't here, either." Suddenly he became serious. "If it isn't here, where the deuce is it?" he mused. "There must *be* a church, because others have seen it; the thing can't walk, not complete with churchyard, ivy and gardens." He was puzzled, and his eyes took on a thoughtful frown. "I'll get to the bottom of this if it takes me all day," he promised himself, and settled down for the search.

For an hour or more he flew up and down the line systematically examining the ground, and was about to abandon his self-appointed task when he came upon it suddenly, and the discovery gave him something of a shock. He was studying a wood, far over the line, which he suspected concealed an archie battery that was worrying him, when his eyes fell on the well-remembered ivy-clad walls, crumbling tombstones and well-kept rectory gardens. It nestled snugly by the edge of the wood, half a mile from a row of tumbledown cottages.

[1] *Home Establishment.*

"So there you are," he muttered grimly. "I'll have a closer look at you and then I'll know you next time I see you." He shoved the stick forward and tore down in a long, screaming dive that brought him to within 1,000 feet of his objective. As he flattened out, his eyes still on the church, he caught his breath suddenly and swerved away. The Camel lurched drunkenly as a stabbing flame split the air and a billow of black smoke blossomed out not thirty yards away. Another appeared in front of him and something smashed through his left wing not a foot from the fuselage. In a moment the air about him was full of vicious jabs of flame and swirling smoke.

"Strewth!" grunted Biggles, as he twisted like a wounded bird in a sea of flying steel and high explosive. "What have I barged into?" He put his nose down until the needle of the speed-indicator rested against the pin, and then, thirty feet from the ground, sped out of the vicinity like a startled snipe.

"Good Lor'!" he said, weakly, as the fusillade died away behind him. "What a mazurka!" He tore across the lines amid a hail of machine-gun bullets, and landing on the aerodrome ran swiftly to the Squadron Office. The C.O., he was told, was in the air. He seized the telephone and called Wing-Headquarters, asking for Colonel Raymond.

"I've found the church, sir," he called, as the Colonel's voice came over the phone. "What about it? I'll tell you. It isn't at Berniet—I beg your pardon, sir—I didn't mean to be impertinent, but it's a fact. It isn't at Bonvillier, either. I spent the morning looking for it and finally ran it to earth on the edge of the oblong-shaped wood just east of Morslede. Funny, did you say, sir? Yes, it's funny; but I've got something still funnier to tell you. That fake tabernacle's on wheels; it moves about after dark—*and the gun you're looking for is inside it*. Just a moment, sir; I'll give you the pin-point. What's that, sir? Shoot! Good! I'll go and watch the fireworks."

Twenty minutes later, from a safe altitude, he watched with marked approval salvo after salvo of shells, hurled by half a dozen batteries of howitzers, tearing the surface off the earth and pounding the "church" and its contents to mangled pulp. An R.E. 8 circled above, doing the "shoot", keeping the gunners on their mark.

"That little lot should teach you to stay put in future," commented Biggles dryly, as he turned for home.

THE ACE OF SPADES

CAPTAIN BIGGLESWORTH of 266 Squadron, R.F.C., known to his friends as "Biggles"; homeward bound from a solitary patrol, glanced casually at the watch on his instrument-board. "Twelve-fifteen," he mused. "Just time to look in and have a word with Wilks before lunch." He altered his course a trifle, and a few minutes later set his Sopwith Camel down neatly on the aerodrome of No. 287 Squadron, where his friend, Captain Wilkinson—more often referred to simply as "Wilks"—commanded a Flight of S.E.5s.

"Is Wilks about?" he called to a group of pilots who were lounging about the entrance to a hangar, in which the dim outlines of some square-nosed S.E.5s could just be seen.

"Hullo, Biggles! Yes, I think he's down in the Mess," was the reply.

"Good enough; I'll stroll down."

"Do you want your tanks filling?"

"No, thanks, laddie; I've plenty to see me home." Biggles tossed his cap and goggles into his cockpit and walked quickly towards the Mess, where he found Wilks, with two or three members of his Flight, indulging in a pre-luncheon aperitif.

"Ah—speak of the devil," declared Wilks.

"Do you often talk about yourself?" inquired Biggles.

"Bah! When are your crowd going to knock a few Huns down?" grinned Wilks.

"Just as soon as the Boche opposite to us have fixed up what few fellows we've left alive with some new machines. Why?"

"We've got seven this week, so far."

"Oh, that's it, is it?" observed Biggles. "Well, you lot so seldom get a Hun that I suppose there is an excuse for you to get a bit chirpy. But you start riding too high on the cock-horse and you'll stall and bruise yourselves. What about providing me with a little refreshment, somebody?"

"The fact is, our new S.E.5s are a bit better than your Camels," explained Wilks apologetically, as he ordered Biggles's drink.

"You think so, eh? Well, let me tell you something. I'd back a Bentley-engined Camel against a long-nosed S.E., as a Hun-getter, any day."

"And let me tell you something," declared Wilks, setting his glass down. "The worst S.E. in this Squadron could make rings round the best Camel you've got—'cos why? Because we've got speed and height on you."

Biggles's eyes glittered. "Well, speed and height aren't everything," he said shortly. "My kite'll turn twice before you're halfway round the first turn. You think that over."

"You'd have to prove that."

"I'll do that."

"How?"

"Camera guns."

"When?"

"Any time you like. Now seems to be the best time; there's no need to wait, as far as I can see."

"How would you arrange it?" inquired Wilks curiously.

"It doesn't need any arranging. We take off with six films each and rendezvous over the aerodrome at ten thousand. No surprise tactics allowed. The show starts as soon as both pilots see each other, and ends as soon as the first man has got his six pictures. Then we'll develop both films and tot up points for hits in the usual way."

"I'll take that on!" cried Wilks, starting up. "I'll show

you whether a perishing, oil-swilling Camel can hold a candle to an S.E."

"Get ready, then. Your jaw will seize up one day, talking too much."

There was a general babble of voices and a move towards the door as everyone hurried out on to the aerodrome to watch the match. "Get one of your fitters to fix me up a gun," Biggles told Wilks.

"I'll see to it."

Ten minutes later the stage was set, and both pilots were ready to climb into their machines.

"Rendezvous over the aerodrome, you said?" queried Wilks.

"That's right; take off how you like. I'll approach from the north and you come in from the south. It doesn't matter about the sun, as the shooting doesn't start until we see each other."

"Good enough."

"Wait a minute, though!" cried Biggles, suddenly remembering something. "Have you got any ammunition in your Vickers?"

"No, they're just being overhauled."

"Hold you hard a minute, then," retorted Biggles. "I've got a full belt in mine and they weigh something. I'll have them taken out and then we'll be square."

It was the work of a moment for a fitter to remove the belt of ammunition, and both machines then took off amid the joyful applause of the assembled aerodrome staff, officers, and ack-emmas.

Biggles headed away to the north, climbing as steeply as possible in order to reach the arranged altitude without loss of time. At eight thousand feet he swung round in a wide circle and headed back towards the aerodrome, knowing that he would be able to make the other two thousand feet by the time he reached it. He peered ahead through his centre-section for the S.E., although he was

still a long way away from the aerodrome, but Wilks
had gone as far to the south as he had to the north, and
they were still invisible to each other.

Biggles, was, of course, backing the manoeuvrability
of the Camel against the slight pull in speed and ceiling
held by the other. He hoped to beat Wilks on the turn,
for the Camel's famous right-hand turn, caused by the
terrific torque of the rotary engine, was a very real advantage in a combat. That was really all he had in his favour,
but it was chiefly upon that quality that he had developed
his own technique in air-fighting, and he hoped to catch
Wilks unprepared for the manoeuvre.

Again he peered ahead for his opponent, and pressed
gently on the rudder-bar to swing his nose clear from the
head-on position. The movement may have saved his life.
There came the shrill clatter of a machine-gun at point-
blank range; at the same moment a stream of tracer poured
between his wings.

The shock was almost stunning in its intensity, so utterly
unprepared was he for anything of the sort, and his actions
for at least two seconds were purely automatic and instinc-
tive. He kicked out his left foot hard, and dragged the joystick back into his right thigh. The Camel bucked like a
wild horse, and before it came out he had recovered his
composure and was looking for his aggressor. He had done
quite a lot of thinking in the brief interval of the half-roll.
His first impression was that Wilks had attacked him,
thinking he had been seen, and by some accident ammunition had been left in his guns. But he dismissed the
thought at once and knew that he had fallen victim to a
prowling Hun, operating for once in a while over the
British side of the lines. That, he reasoned, could only
mean that the Hun—if Hun it was—was an old hand at
the game; a novice would hardly dare to take such a
risk.

If it was so, then he was by no means out of the wood.

for, unarmed, he could only make for the ground, an operation that would require a few minutes of time, a period of which the Hun, finding his fire was not returned, would certainly take full advantage.

Then he saw him, an orange-and-black Fokker D.VIII, with a large Ace of Spades painted on the side of its fuselage. Biggles brought the Camel round in a lightning turn that put him on the tail of the black-crossed machine for a few seconds. Automatically he sighted his guns and growled when his pressure on the Bowden lever produced no results. At that moment he thought he could have got his man, but there was no time for idle speculation. The Hun had reversed the position by a clever move, and a tattered skylight warned Biggles that he had better follow the old adage of running away if he wished to fight again another day.

He spun, counted six turns, and came out. Instantly the chatter of guns sounded so close that he winced. He held the Camel in a dizzy turn for a minute, with the Hun racing behind him trying to bring his guns to bear, and then he spun again. All the time, at the back of his mind, was a fierce condemnation of his utter and inexcusable folly in flying without ammunition, and an equally fierce conviction that if he did succeed in reaching the ground alive he would never again be guilty of such madness. He spun for so long that he became giddy, and pulled out sluggishly. But the Hun was still with him, and he heard his bullets ripping through the spruce and canvas of his fuselage.

For the first time in his life he nearly panicked. He twisted and turned like a minnow with a pike on its tail, losing height on every possible occasion, and finally sideslipping steeply into a field that appeared invitingly under him. He did not notice that a narrow ditch ran diagonally across the field, and it would have made no difference if he had. Fortunately, the Camel had nearly run to a stop when he reached it, so it suffered no serious damage. It lurched sickeningly, stopped dead, and cocked its tail up into the air. The prop disintegrated into flying splinters, mixed with clods of earth.

Biggles jerked forward and struck his nose on the padded ends of his guns with a force that made him "see stars". He undid his safety-belt, and looked up just in time to see the Hun waving him an ironic farewell. He watched it disappear into the distance, followed by a long trail of archie bursts, and then climbed out on to the ground to survey the damage. As he did so, he noticed for the first time that a road bounded the field, over the hedge of which a number of Tommies were grinning at him. He heard a car pull up with a grinding of brakes, but he paid no attention to it until a sharp commanding voice brought him round with a jerk. No fewer than three red-tabbed officers were coming towards him; the first, an elderly, hard-faced man, wore the badges of a General.

"My gosh! Here's a General come to sympathise with me. I couldn't bear it," muttered Biggles to himself, and he was framing a suitable reply when the General spoke. The voice was not sympathetic. In fact, there was something in the tone of voice that made him wince, and may have resulted in his subsequent attitude.

"How long have you been in France?" began the General, coldly.

"About eleven months, sir," answered Biggles.

"That seems to have been quite long enough."

Biggles stared, hardly able to believe his ears. Then, suddenly understanding the implication behind the General's words, he froze, and clenched his teeth.

"I witnessed the whole affair—I'd hardly call it a combat —from start to finish," went on the General contemptuously. "Not once did you make the slightest attempt to return the German's fire. In fact, to put the matter still more clearly, you ran away. Am I right?"

"Quite right, sir," answered Biggles frostily.

"I thought so. That orange-and-black Fokker has been causing a lot of trouble over our side of the lines lately, and you had an admirable opportunity to shoot him down, such an opportunity that may not occur again. It is a pity you did not take advantage of it, but it would seem that he was the better man."

"It would seem so, sir."

"It would be futile to deny it," went on the General, icily. "What is your name?"

"Bigglesworth, sir."

"Squadron?"

"Two-six-six, sir."

"At Maranique, I believe."

"That is so, sir."

"Very well. Report back to your unit at once."

"Very good, sir."

The General turned on his heel, closely followed by his two *aides*. Biggles watched them go, sullen anger smouldering in his eyes. "Never been in the air in your lives, any of you, I'll bet. You'd jump like cats if you heard a gun go off. Then, without asking why, you come and call me a coward," he mused. "The fact is, I suppose that Hun has been shooting up your snug little headquarters, and you don't like it. You wouldn't. Well, I hope he blows your dug-out as high as the Eiffel Tower, and I hope you're inside it when he does," he concluded, as he made his way slowly down the road in search of a telephone, to ask for transport to fetch him, and the wrecked Camel, home.

II

Major Mullen's opening remark when, an hour later, he reported at the Squadron Office, was an inopportune one, particularly with Biggles in his present mood. Far from pouring oil on troubled waters, it added fuel to a conflagration.

"You've let me down badly, Bigglesworth," he began.

Biggles drew a deep breath, and stiffened. This sort of talk from the General had merely irritated him, but that his own C.O. should doubt him put him in a cold fury.

"You let a Hun run you into the ground without firing a shot at him." The Major did not ask a question; he made a statement, and Biggles, who was about to explain the true facts of the case, shut up like an oyster. He made no reply.

"You've broken your machine, I hear," went on the C.O.

"I have, sir."

"Brigadier-General Sir Hales-Morier, of Air Headquarters, has just been on the phone to me. I will spare your feelings by not repeating what he said, but I gather he proposes to post you to Home Establishment; in the meantime, he wants a report tonight from me on the matter. It is to reach him by 6.30, so will you please make out your own report and let me have it by five o'clock."

"I will, sir."

"That's all."

Biggles did not go to the Mess. Instead, seething with anger, he made his way moodily to the sheds. He stood on the deserted tarmac for a few minutes and then sent an ack-emma down to the Mess with a message to Algy Lacey, of his own Flight, informing him that he was borrowing his machine and would be back some time. Then he took off and hedge-hopped—finding some satisfaction in the risks he took—to 287 Squadron, and told Wilks, whom he found at lunch, just what had occurred.

Wilks, who was about to pull Biggles's leg in connection with his failure to turn up at the appointed place, whistled. "What are you going to do about it?" he asked.

"Do? Nothing—not a blessed thing."

"You might have told your Old Man about only having celluloid in your guns."

"I'm making no excuses to anybody; people can think what they like. Brass-hats should either ask why, or look at a fellow's record before they jump down his throat, and mine isn't too bad, although I say it myself."

"They'll think you've lost your nerve and send you home," observed Wilks, soberly.

"Let 'em. I'd as soon be busted by a hamfisted pupil at an F.T.S.[1] as have my inside perforated by explosive bullets. We'll be able to finish that little duel sometime when you come home on leave."

"Don't talk rot. You go and tell Mullen that you hadn't any ammunition, or I will."

"You mind your own blooming business, Wilks," Biggles told him coldly, and refusing an invitation to stay to lunch returned to his Camel.

He swept into the air in a climbing turn, so steep that if his engine had conked the story of his war exploits would have ended there and then; he knew it perfectly well, and derived a bitter sort of satisfaction from the knowledge. But his engine continued to give full revs., and on a wide throttle he climbed in ever-increasing circles. He knew precisely where he was, for as one landmark disappeared from view he picked out another, although this procedure was purely automatic, and demanded no conscious thought. Yet where he was going he did not know; he was simply flying for the sake of flying. In his present frame of mind he had no desire to talk to anyone, least of all his own Squadron. So he continued to climb, thinking about the affair of the morning.

It was a burst of white archie about two hundred yards ahead that brought him out of his reverie. It was only a single burst, and as it was British archie it could only mean one thing—a signal. Mentally thanking the gunners for

[1] *Flying Training School.*

what should have been quite unnecessary, he scanned the sky around quickly for the hostile machine that he knew must be in the vicinity, and was just in time to see a vague shadow disappear into the eye of the sun. It had gone too quickly for him to recognise the type, but as he could see no other machines in the sky, he assumed it was an enemy.

Now, a newcomer to the game would have turned at once, and thus made it clear to the stalker—if stalker it was—that he had been observed; but Biggles did nothing of the sort. He did certain things quickly, but he held straight on his course. The first thing he did was to pull up the handle of his C.C. gear and fire two or three shots to satisfy himself that the guns were working; then he twisted round in his seat as far as his thick flying-kit and the cramped space would permit, and squinted through his extended fingers in the direction of the sun. The glare was blinding, but by just keeping the ball of the thumb over the blazing disc and opening his fingers only wide enough to get a blurred view through the bristles of his gauntlet he was able to search the danger zone. He picked out a straight-winged machine, in silhouette, end-on, and knew that the enemy pilot was just launching his attack.

Not by a single movement of joystick or rudder did he reveal that he had spotted the attacker. He watched its approach. Only when the Hun, who now appeared as a thick black spot, was about three hundred yards away did he push his joystick forward for more speed; then, when he judged that the other was about to fire, he made a lightning Immelmann turn. He knew that at that moment the enemy pilot would be squinting through his sights, and the disappearance of the Camel from his limited field of view would not unduly alarm him.

In this he was apparently correct. The Boche, no doubt thinking he had a "sitter", wasted three precious seconds looking for him in his sights, and it was the sharp stutter of Biggles's guns that warned him of his peril and sent him half-volleying wildly.

Now it is a curious fact that, although Biggles had been thinking about his orange-and-black acquaintance of the morning when the archie gunners had fired their well-timed shot, all thought of him went out of his head when he realised that he was being stalked; so it was with something of a mild shock, swiftly followed by savage exultation, that he saw the well-remembered colours through his sights as he took the Hun broadside on and grabbed his Bowden lever.

The pilot of the black-crossed machine came out of his life-saving manoeuvre, looking around with a speed born of long experience. He saw the Camel anywhere but where he expected to find it, and in the last place he hoped to find it—on his tail. But he was, as Biggles had assumed, no novice at the game, and did not allow the British machine to retain the coveted position long enough to do him any harm. Biggles did actually get in a quick burst just as the other machine darted out of his sights, but it was ineffective, and the duel began in earnest, both pilots aware that it could only end in the downfall of one of them.

They were evenly matched, although Biggles, smarting from his reprimand of the morning—for which, rightly or wrongly, he blamed the pilot of the orange machine—fought with a ferocity that would not have been possible in a normal cold-blooded battle. He hit the other machine several times, but without causing it any apparent damage, and he took several shots through his own empennage in return.

The fight had opened over the British side of the lines, the Hun evidently repeating his tactics of the morning; but a fairly strong wind was carrying both machines towards the pock-marked barren strip of no-man's-land. Naturally, this was not to Biggles's liking, for unless the

Hun made a bad mistake, which was hardly to be expected, he would soon be fighting with enemy territory below. So, gambling on the Hun repeating the tactics he had followed during the encounter of the morning, he deliberately spun. As he hoped, the other machine followed him. Twisting his head round, he could see the Hun spinning down behind him. He counted six turns, came out, and instantly spun the other way. This time, however, he allowed the machine to make only one turn. He pulled it out into a loop, half rolled on to even keel on top of the loop, and to his intense satisfaction saw the Hun go spinning past him. The short spin had caught him off his guard, and as he came out, Biggles thrust home his attack. He deliberately held his fire until it was impossible to miss, and then fired one of the longest bursts he had ever fired in his life.

The Hun jerked upwards, fell off on to his wing, and spun. Biggles was taking no chances. He followed him down without taking his eyes off him for an instant, in case it was a ruse. But it was no ruse. The orange Fokker went nose-first into the ground with its engine full on, and Biggles stiffened in his seat as he watched that fearful crash. He circled for a minute or two, looking for a suitable place to land. It was not his usual practice to look at unpleasant sights too closely, but on this occasion an idea had struck him, and he had a definite object in view.

With people hurrying towards the crash from all points of the compass he put the Camel down in an adjacent field and joined the hurrying crowd. His great fear was that the wreck would be removed piecemeal by souvenir-hunters before he could reach it, but he found an officer on the spot when he got there, and the machine lay exactly as it had fallen.

III

It was five o'clock when he reported to the Squadron Office.

Major Mullen looked up from his desk as he entered. "Ah, you've brought your report," he said.

"Er—yes, sir."

"Good. First of all, though, you had better read what I have said. Here is the minute; I shall attach your report to it."

Biggles took the buff sheet and felt his face go red with shame as he read a eulogy of his conduct and exploits since he had joined the Squadron. The C.O., he knew, must have gone to considerable trouble in the matter, for he had looked up a large number of combat reports—not all his own—and pinned them to the document. Further, he had evidently been in communication with Major Paynter, for a lengthy report from his old C.O. was also attached.

Biggles did not read it all through, but laid it on the C.O.'s desk. "Thank you, sir," he said quietly, "but I'm afraid I don't deserve such praise."

"That is for me to decide," replied the C.O. Then, with a quick change of tone, he added, "What on earth possessed you to behave like that this morning, and before such an audience, too?"

A slow smile spread over Biggles's face. "Well, the fact of the matter is, sir," he said sheepishly, "I was in the air without any ammunition. It sounds silly, I know, but I had arranged to fight a camera-gun duel with Wilks—that is, Wilkinson, of 287, who claimed that his S.E. was better than my Camel."

"Then why, in the name of heaven, didn't you tell that interfering old fool—no, I don't mean that—why didn't you tell the General so?"

Biggles shrugged his shoulders. "I find it hard to argue with people who form their own opinions before they know the facts."

"Like that, was it?"

"Just like that, sir!"

"I see. Well, let me have your report."

"I'm afraid it's rather a bulky one, sir," replied Biggles, struggling with something under his tunic.

The C.O. stared in wide-eyed amazement. "What in the name of goodness have you got there?" he gasped.

Biggles slowly unfolded a large sheet of orange fabric on which was painted a Maltese Cross and beside it an Ace of Spades. He laid it on the C.O.'s desk. "That, sir, is the hide of the hound who made me bust my Camel this morning. I chanced to meet him again this afternoon, and on that occasion I had lead in my guns. I think H.Q. will recognise that Ace of Spades, and perhaps it will speak plainer than words. I'm not much of a hand with a pen, anyway."